SHOWDOWN AT THE OLD MILL

A PRATT DEMPCY & COMPANY
WESTERN ADVENTURE – BOOK 4

INSPIRED BY TRUE EVENTS

ORRIS SLADE

Publisher's Note: This is a work of fiction. Names, characters, places and incidents are a product of the author's imagination. Locales and public names are sometimes used for atmospheric purposes. Any resemblance to actual people, living or dead, or to businesses, companies, events, institutions, or locales is completely coincidental.

Contents

Prologue

December 1880

Timber, California

The cold seeped into his bones as he leaned over the table. Sun-kissed, scarred fingers circled a bottle of beer. He tipped it back and took a big swig, feeling the knot in his gut ease with each gulp.

Budd Mansfield was a man on the run. He kept his voice low and his head even lower, trying not to draw attention to himself as patrons spilled in through the saloon doors. A gust of frigid air blew through the saloon each time someone stepped inside. He turned up the collar of his coat and shuddered.

Folks knew him around here, but in Timber, no one dared to call out for the lawmen. Everyone in this godforsaken town had their pockets filled with dirty money. Most of it from Ripley Eagleson.

Still, Budd tried his hardest to blend in, even as his enormous frame drew more than a couple of stares in his direction. He sipped at his beer and listened to the deep drawl of Blake Wright's voice as he droned on about his brothers, Charles and Steven. Evan Farris had said something in response, but Budd barely heard any of the conversation over the sound of his own guilty conscience.

There was an odd numbness that had settled over him. A numbness that meant a part of him had died when he found himself branded as an outlaw.

Whether it was pride or sheer stubbornness that kept him on a straight path in the past, he wasn't sure, but Budd had always seen himself as more than just a bandit with a twisted sense of justice.

"Budd?" Blake whispered. "You all right?"

Budd shook his head. "I don't know if it's this cold weather or the looks we're getting in here, but I got a bad feeling nagging at me."

"You always got a bad feeling." Evan snorted. "What's it about this time?"

Budd shifted in his seat and gulped down the rest of his beer. He slid the bottle to the edge of the table and sighed. "I ain't too sure. Just got the feeling someone's watching me. Can't shake it."

Evan, Blake, and the former sheriff, Dawson, looked around the room with the same suspicion in their gazes that he felt. They were all wanted men hiding in plain sight. Life hadn't been easy since they broke out of the jailhouse. Last thing they needed was someone on their trail.

"See those men over there?" Budd asked as he gestured toward a nearby table. "They have been giving us side glances since we walked in."

"Take it easy, Budd..." Dawson warned.

But Budd was tired of feeling like he was being watched. He shook his head and tapped his knuckles on the table.

The saloon girl carried over another round of beers for them before she scurried away. She left with a smile and a wink. Budd glanced away uncomfortably and turned his attention back to the conversation.

"We have been on the road for two weeks now," he grumbled. "I suppose it's just getting to me. That's all."

Evan and the others relaxed a bit. They looked to him with unwavering loyalty, and it frightened Budd. It was because of him why they were just as wanted as he was.

He had failed to prove that Ripley Eagleson was the culprit behind a series of attacks on the Pratt & Dempcy stagecoach company. Because of Budd, the four of them sat in a lonely saloon with the weight of the world on their shoulders.

"Ain't that Budd Mansfield?" said the man from two tables over. He wobbled in his chair a bit, but he looked just sober enough to cause trouble.

Budd glanced up and locked eyes with the drunken fool. A spark of recognition passed between them, and Budd panicked. He shot the man a warning glare that went unnoticed.

The stranger nudged his pal, and the two of them whispered. Fingers pointed in his direction. Bile crawled up the back of Budd's throat, burning his tongue and leaving a foul taste in his mouth.

"It is. It's Budd Mansfield."

Before he knew it, Budd was on his feet. He grabbed the man by the back of his shirt and dragged him through the back door. A fist flew toward Budd's face, and he leaped out of the way. "Keep my name out of your mouth," he snarled. "I ain't going to tell you twice, friend."

"You ain't my friend," the man spat. He swung for Budd again, just as his drinking companion followed them through the door.

The second man grabbed Budd, holding him still as punches rained down upon him.

"We can talk this out!" Budd hollered.

"Ain't no talkin' to a killer," said the man as he punched Budd once again.

Budd struggled. He kicked out, and his boot landed square in the center of the first man's chest. The man stumbled back. Budd used all his strength and shook off the crushing grip around his middle.

Thick, greasy hands scrambled for purchase, but Budd broke free. He rammed his elbow into the fool's nose, and blood sprayed onto the ground.

The first man recovered from the kick and jumped onto Budd's back. Fingers dug into his eyes, but he clawed them away. He heard a howl of pain and blinked past the burning in his hazy vision.

Budd swung his fist, which connected with the man's jaw. His sight cleared, and he took in the image of the two battered men in the alley.

"Forget my face," he said gravely. "Both of you. I mean it. Or else you'll have more than a broken nose and cracked jaw to deal with."

Chapter 1

Sacramento, California

Darkness fell over the city as Ripley Eagleson strolled toward the mayor's office. He pushed his way through the door and tipped his hat to the young lady behind the front desk. She smiled nervously and led him through another set of doors. Mayor Thomas stood beside a large window and looked out at the bustling streets of Sacramento.

Ripley cleared his throat and approached the man slowly. "Any word from your connections in Reno?" he asked.

"No. No sign of Mansfield anywhere." The mayor sighed. His shoulders slumped over in defeat. "I should have seen it sooner. The signs were there all along."

"Budd Mansfield killed my own brother-in-law. Take it from me. There was nothing you could have done to change what happened." Rip made a show of dabbing the corner of his eye with a handkerchief. He tucked the cloth into his pocket and took a seat near the mayor's desk. "What about Mr. Thayer? Has his memory returned yet?"

Mayor Thomas shook his head. "He only recalls Mansfield and Blake Wright."

Rip bit down on the inside of his cheek and kept himself from smiling victoriously. After all, he had caused Mr. Thayer's recent bout of memory loss. He had intended to kill the man, but he was pleased with how things developed.

His gang was free. He had successfully exacted revenge on Pratt & Dempcy, and he held Budd Mansfield's fate in the palm of his hand. Life, it seemed, was good. All he needed to do was make sure Mansfield stayed out of Sacramento and out of his way.

Since the jailbreak, there'd been no sign of Mansfield anywhere in the region. As a man who spent his life hunting outlaws, Mansfield had proven himself to be just as slippery as any crook or criminal Rip knew.

There was something poetic about it, really. And the thought of such a bittersweet ending to Budd Mansfield's story just tickled Ripley. He was almost disappointed their little game of cat and mouse had to end.

"We are all mourning those lost in the attack on the city," Ripley sighed. "But we must help the marshal bring down the men responsible."

As if summoned by name, Marshal Eddison Greene entered the mayor's office. He removed his hat and eyed Rip with suspicion burning in his emerald gaze. The lawman meant business, and it was clear to Rip that Greene wasn't too eager to just write Budd Mansfield off as the culprit. "Let's get this meeting underway, gentlemen," said Greene. "Unless you would rather hold this gathering at another time?"

"No, no. I would very much like to put an end to all of this," Rip replied. "These few years have been quite traumatic for me—as you can imagine."

"In what way?" Greene's expression was impassive, blank in a way that was most unsettling.

"Well… being blamed for crimes I didn't commit, for one." Rip slumped forward and frowned deeply. "Not to mention having to hide my identity for so long."

"In the time you spent under Budd Mansfield's control, why didn't you attempt to reach out for help?" Greene asked. "Why not go to the law? Or even Mayor Thomas?"

"I-I was afraid. Sheriff Dawson was being paid by Mansfield. I couldn't ask for help."

The marshal dropped his hat onto the mayor's desk and crossed his arms over his chest. "And what about before he arrived in Sacramento? How do you explain the crimes committed by the Blood Eagle Gang?"

"I can't tell you what I don't know," Rip whined. "I only know about the stagecoach attacks he blamed me for."

Marshal Greene cocked his head to the side and chewed his bottom lip. "That does not sound good for you. A contact in Chicago has stated Budd Mansfield finished a contract for the Pinkertons only months before he arrived in Sacramento. That means he wasn't in California for five of the stagecoach robberies or the crimes that predate Pratt and Dempcy's move to the territory."

"What does that have to do with me?" Rip asked.

"You tell me, Mr. Eagleson," the lawman scoffed. "Someone led that gang before Mansfield. Someone who helped the bandits escape the jailhouse."

"Are you implying I am responsible?"

"No," Mayor Thomas answered in the marshal's stead. "Of course he isn't. It's just the marshal's job to ask these sorts of questions."

Rip was peeved. He smoothed a hand over his suit. Though the motion straightened out the fabric, it revealed a fracture in his carefully sculpted facade. A fracture that the marshal had not hesitated to exploit with his questions.

Luckily, Rip could regain a bit of his control when the lawman let something slip. According to the U.S. Marshal's contacts in the region, Budd Mansfield had a somewhat colorful past.

"What do you mean by colorful past?" Rip asked while he feigned shock. "Has he done these sorts of crimes before?"

"No," replied the marshal. "Nothing like this. But I know the Pinkertons had trouble keeping Mansfield in line. The man has a temper. He was relieved of his contractual obligations with the Pinkertons after throttling a man half to death. Apparently, Mansfield disagreed with a judge's decision when an outlaw was declared innocent."

Rip stored the information away in his mind, intending to give it more thought later. "So it's not impossible to believe he's capable of the crimes he's being charged with?"

"Not... impossible," said the marshal. "But unlikely."

"Still, you have to admit he's a violent man. A man who has the skills to rob stagecoaches and—"

The marshal held his hand up, silencing Rip's words. "Whoever robbed the stagecoaches was careful," he inserted. "But they were sloppy with the killings. None of the murders seemed planned. Hopefully, the notes left behind by the deputies will help me sort this out. In the meantime..." The marshal stood up a little straighter and loomed over Rip. "I suggest you don't leave town."

***

Timber, California

The shadows of the corridor wrapped around Budd like a shroud. He allowed the darkness to embrace him as he crept closer to the room. He lifted his hand and hesitated for a moment. His presence was likely to put a good friend in danger, but Budd had no other choice.

Ginger answered after three knocks. Her copper curls bounced when she popped her head out the crack in the door. The soiled dove flashed a toothy grin when she spotted him and opened the door wider.

"My, my. If it ain't Budd Mansfield himself knockin' on my door," she murmured. "To what do I owe this pleasure? You ain't here to try to save me from a life of debauchery again, are you?" Her chuckle echoed in the empty hallway.

Budd allowed himself a small smile as he shook his head and stepped inside Ginger's bedchamber. "I've known you for as long as I've been in California. You might know me better than anyone else. These things they're saying about me in the papers... they ain't true."

"I know."

"Then you understand why I need your help again," he sighed. "Ripley Eagleson is trying to pin the stagecoach robberies on me, and I can't let that happen. I need you to be my eyes and ears in Timber."

"Rip comes through the town every week." Ginger shut the door and walked across the room. She peeked through the gap in the curtains. "He stays at the hotel. Always arrives alone, but the ladies have heard other voices coming from the room."

"Do you think his gang is in town?"

"Hector Vasquez showed his face in the saloon three days ago, Budd," Ginger said, with a touch of pity in her voice. "I know you worked hard to put them away, but not much has changed around these parts."

Budd sat down on the edge of Ginger's bed and scrubbed a hand over his face. He sighed heavily, exhausted from his new life on the run. "I need your help. We can't set things right if Eagleson is always a step ahead of us."

"You know I owe you my life. There ain't nothin' I wouldn't do for you after you saved me." Ginger sat beside Budd and patted his hand. "I'll keep an eye on things."

Budd remembered the day he met Ginger. She had been traveling with her sister when their stagecoach was attacked by the Blood Eagle Gang and Ripley Eagleson. Sadly, Ginger's sister had been killed in the crossfire.

Budd carried the young woman to town and tried in vain to save her. He was grateful Ginger had never blamed him for her sister's death. Instead, the two of them had bonded in their grief.

"You ain't the only one waitin' for the day Ripley Eagleson is hanged," Ginger said vehemently. "I'll do what I can for you, Budd. Good luck."

Budd pressed a kiss to Ginger's forehead and took his leave.

He made his way down the hall of the inn once more. Budd entered his room quietly and found Dawson was awake. "Are the others still asleep?" he asked before he cleared his throat.

His answer came as a snore from the corner of the room. Evan slept upright, with his back to the wall and a gun clutched in his hand. Blake was on the bed. His knife tucked beneath the pillow. Both men looked ready to attack at any minute. Budd reckoned he hadn't looked much different when he slept the night through.

"I was wrong, you know," Dawson said suddenly. "About you, I mean. I always gave you a hard time. Now I'm wondering, if I had just stayed out of the way, none of this would have happened. Maybe you would have caught Eagleson a long time ago."

"No use in getting hung up on something like that. Time passes. We learn our lessons. That's all we can hope for," Budd replied. He sat across from Dawson at the table and folded his hands on the surface. "Is that what's keeping you awake?"

Dawson shook his head and ran his fingers through his hair. "Just thinking about Norma. We haven't been married a year yet, and she has to deal with this. She must face all sorts of slander and ridicule back in Sacramento."

"She's safe with your father," Budd said, although he wasn't sure why he sought to comfort the disgraced lawman. He had once envied Dawson for his wife and family. However, he realized at that moment that Dawson's greatest strength was also his greatest weakness. He respected Dawson, but they weren't exactly friends.

It was circumstance that caused their destinies to become intertwined and nothing more. Still, Budd saw they had a common enemy and extended a hand to Dawson. Their little band of outcasts wasn't much, but it was the closest thing to family Budd had ever known.

"What about Dorothy Valentine?" Dawson asked with a hint of amusement in his voice.

"What about her?"

"Ain't you worried Ripley Eagleson might try to—"

"Dotty can handle herself," Budd insisted. Though he had wondered if she was safe in Reno. After all, she had a bad habit of finding trouble where there wasn't any. "I trust her father put certain things in place to ensure her safety after his death. Either way, Dotty has no use for a man like me. I'm sure her feelings were nothing more than a passing fancy. She'll soon forget me."

Dawson picked up his cup and sipped something dark and bitter before he spoke again. "I wish no harm to her or any of you. Lord knows, you've proven yourselves enough by now, but I... just can't let something like this happen again. I took your word that nothing bad would happen if I allowed Evan and the others to help with your investigation. Your association with outlaws got me tossed in that cell beside you. Don't make me regret trusting you, Budd."

"When we prove Ripley Eagleson is guilty, I hope you see that putting your faith in me wasn't the wrong choice," Budd sighed.

Chapter 2

The following morning arrived with the pale yellow glow of the rising sun. A blanket of fog slithered across the ground, obscuring the roads.

Folks hurried to begin the day's work. Wagons rolled on with a rattle and a squeak. And Budd Mansfield's bloodshot gaze watched it through the shutters of a window.

He hadn't slept a wink. In fact, his wandering mind hadn't allowed him a good night's rest in over a week. Not when they had gotten closer to a plan to infiltrate the Old Mill. He just needed a little more time. But time was something they had run out of a long time ago.

"Stop thinking he's one step ahead of us. Instead, think of it like we're only one step behind him. Hell, we're practically breathing down the back of his neck," Evan grumbled to Blake, who had been brooding in the corner. "Ripley Eagleson won't know what hit him when we take him down from the inside."

"That's *if* we can get inside," retorted Blake.

Evan didn't seem deterred by his friend's irritable tone. He waved his hand dismissively. "Budd's got it all figured out. Trust the man with a plan, and things will go off without a hitch."

Dawson entered the room just then. He slammed the morning paper onto the table and paced the floor. Budd made his way over. He scowled down at the headline that claimed he had orchestrated the jailbreak on his own. It seemed Ripley Eagleson was busy slandering him.

"We're all mentioned by name," Dawson hissed. "Eventually, not even Timber will be safe for us."

Evan and Blake's bickering came to a halt. The two men had been outlaws in the past and had easily slipped back into the life of wanted men, while Budd and Dawson struggled. They took the news in stride about the article in the paper.

Evan grabbed it from the table and read aloud, "Citizens of Sacramento fear the ruthless gang may strike again."

Budd snapped his fingers as a thought occurred. He walked over to his bag and grabbed a map of the region that he bought off a trapper. His fingers traced the roads leading out of Sacramento. "That's it," he exclaimed. "Ripley told the paper the people of *Sacramento* fear another attack. Not Timber or any of the other settlements in the territory."

"So?" scoffed Blake.

"So that means the Blood Eagles will attack one of these roads soon, and Ripley Eagleson will try to pin it on us," Budd explained. "It's a performance, a show to earn the marshal's favor."

Dawson nearly leaped into the air with excitement. "And when the gang strikes, there will be a fresh trail to the Old Mill we can follow."

Budd nodded his head and said, "We create a distraction to draw the men away and search for the ledger. Once we have it, we send word to Steven in Reno to approach Beatrice." It was as good a plan as any. Budd felt hope spark inside of him for the first time since they broke free from the jailhouse. They had a chance to set things right, and he refused to let it pass him by.

"I can cause a distraction." Blake pointed to a spot near a quarry. "There's an old cache up here from before the miners cleared out of the area. Should have some explosives I can use."

Budd used a pen and marked the quarry cache. "All right. You can head to the cache tomorrow. The rest of us will patrol the roads each night until the attack. Meet us back here by Wednesday, and we'll head for the Old Mill."

They assigned the men a road on the map before Budd folded it back up and tucked it safely in his pocket. He then called his allies to the table for one last conversation before the day's work started.

"This ain't gonna be easy. The plan might not even work," he said. "So I will not judge any man here who wishes to count his blessings that we're still alive and head for the border."

The men fell silent.

Budd practically heard the wheels grinding in their heads. He stood tall at the center of the room with a steaming cup of coffee in his hand. There was no shame or regret in his gaze, and he hoped the others felt the same.

He hoped they wanted to fight to prove they were innocent. And he held onto that hope like it was the only thing that mattered anymore.

"I'm with you to the end, partner," Evan chuckled. "There's no way I'm giving you all the glory. Besides, I wager seeing Ripley Eagleson's smile slide off that smug face of his will be a grand old time."

Blake and Dawson looked as though they were considering Budd's offer. They both had their reasons, and Budd was sure if Steven had been there, he would have considered it too. Not that Budd would have blamed them for running when they had the chance. He just simply wasn't the sort of man who chose freedom over justice.

Even if he never cleared his name, Budd was determined to see Ripley Eagleson pay for his crimes.

"My brother's gang is responsible for this mess," said Blake finally. "It's only right that I help you. After all, you gave me a chance when no one else would."

Dawson clapped Budd on the shoulder. The former lawman gave Budd a sheepish grin and said, "I'm with you."

***

The Old Mill

With a groan, the gate swung open. The scent of rusted metal and roasting meat permeated from the gaps in the walls.

Four men waited near the entrance of the decrepit old fort. Hector Vasquez, Salazar Torez, Charles Wright, and the leader of the bandit camp close to the Old Mill took a step closer. Ripley Eagleson nodded to the men as he passed them by and handed his horse off to a servant. Storm fussed the second his rider was out of his line of sight.

Rip stretched high above his head as his men approached. He could tell by the way their hands twitched they were looking to satisfy some barbaric urges. "Gentlemen, I come with good news," he announced. "I believe I am well on my way to bringing Mayor Thomas over to our side. Once we have his loyalty, we have his city."

Hector Vasquez and the others looked uncertain, but Salazar looked downright furious. He separated from the group and spoke up. "They promised us riches, gold and silver, and more women. Instead, we sit here for weeks waiting for what? News that we are *almost* ready for another job?"

"Have you not seen the treasures we've acquired over the years?" Rip snapped. "Have I not provided for your families and loved ones while you are under my employment?"

"No one is sayin' you don't provide," said Charles. "Salazar and the rest of us are just tired of livin' like animals while you walk around in your fancy suits and sip brandy with the mayor. We're supposed to be runnin' this territory, but we're hidin' out like yellow-bellied cowards. That ain't how it was supposed to go."

Anger surged inside of Rip. Ungrateful. All of them were ungrateful fools.

"I am trying to make us free men, to give us lives we were told we weren't worthy of."

"Your way of doing things does not work anymore. It got Leroy captured and got Johnny killed," Salazar spat. He broke into a string of curses and Spanish that Rip couldn't understand. "I am tired of following you."

None of the men moved. They stood in shock at Salazar's defiance.

Rip reached down and pulled the knife from his boot. He stabbed the knife into Salazar's arm and twisted the blade until the outlaw dropped to his knees with a shriek.

Rip tore Salazar's gun free from its holster and pressed it against the outlaw's skull. He remained calm and proper, as if Salazar's blood had not stained his hand.

"We take Sacramento when I say so," he stated. "And I will not tolerate any insubordination. Do I make myself clear?"

"¡Lo siento! ¡Lo siento!" Sal wailed.

Charles, Hector, and the bandit leader all nodded their heads. Sal gritted his teeth as Rip yanked the knife free. The outlaw toppled over. Bandits rushed over to aid him as Rip whistled a jaunty tune.

He wiped the blood from his knife and watched as Sal cradled his wounded arm. The bandits propped Sal up against the wall of the Old Mill and fetched the doctor.

"Clean him up and send him into my office. I'm tired of being questioned." Rip pulled Hector aside and led him into the building.

They entered the cavernous space that served as their hideaway.

Rip grabbed a rag from the table and cleaned the blood from his hand as he sat down. He propped his legs up onto the table, crossing them at the ankle. "Do you want to tell me why you have failed to find Pete Jones's body?"

"I checked the plot of unmarked graves and found nothing, boss," Hector told Rip. "If he's dead, he is not in Sacramento."

"The town buries outlaws in that plot outside of town. If he's dead, he's there. Look again. I want to send his body back to his family."

"But we already—"

Rip threw his feet down and stood up so quickly that the chair fell over. He glared down at Hector and sneered, "I don't care what you already did. Do as I say."

"Yes, sir."

"Good," he retorted as he picked the chair up and sat down with the usual air of superiority that hovered around him like a thick smog. "Now tell me who the new leader of the camp is. Last I checked, we weren't looking to promote anyone."

"Isiah West," Hector replied. "He used to steal cattle and sell them for more than they were worth. Now he robs anything on wheels. Isiah killed the last bandit in charge of the camp and staked his claim over the men."

"Salazar must have loved that." Rip chuckled and retrieved a cigar from his breast pocket. He struck a match against the table and lit the end of his cigar.

"Bring him with us on the next job. We could use a little more ruthless aggression in our ranks. Some of the men seem to be getting a little… soft." Rip stared pointedly at Hector. "Do what you want to them, but no killing. We don't need the marshal getting suspicious. Fetch the others."

"Yes, sir." Hector disappeared through the door.

He then emerged with the rest of the gang.

Isiah West strayed closer to Rip than Salazar or Charles. The bandit leader had an energy about him that resonated with Rip. "What's the job?" Isiah asked. "All I need to know is who I'm robbin' and how much I'm gettin' paid."

"Three hundred."

Isiah whistled before a sly grin overcame his expression. "Sounds like tomorrow will be a good day. I'm ready to go when you are, boss."

"You have an hour to prepare, and then we head to Calligan Road," Rip chuckled. "There's a wagon stocked with mercantile goods and a bank deposit. Fence the goods in Timber and bring the money to me. Keep a cool head, and I might just consider using you for future jobs."

Chapter 3

Calligan Road

Sacramento, California

The smell of rain clung to the air as a storm approached. Wind rustled Sal's long hair, blowing it wildly around his face. But he paid it no mind. He locked his gaze on the hills in the distance. The wagon was scheduled to arrive in Sacramento at any minute.

"Hey, Sal."

"What is it, gringo?"

"Why isn't Rip on this job with us?" Isiah grumbled. Everyone realized Isiah was looking to impress their boss.

"Someone had to keep the lawmen busy." Salazar led the three men along the path that merged onto Calligan Road. He flexed his fingers and felt the stitches in his arm tug. Half of him wished he had ripped the knife out of his arm and buried it in Rip's chest when he had the chance. But Lord knew Ripley Eagleson was too stubborn to let something like that kill him, not when Sal still owed him a debt.

"So what's your story?" asked Isiah. "How'd you get wrapped up in all this?"

Sal glanced over his shoulder at the bandit leader.

"I chose a life of violence. I am not so different from anyone else," he answered. "I like power, so I take it."

"You like bein' an outlaw?"

"Do you?"

"No." Isiah eyed Sal suspiciously. "I don't know an outlaw under my command that chose this life. Circumstances make good men criminals."

"It is a man's choice that makes him a criminal," Sal said as he unsheathed his favorite knife and flipped it into the air before catching it between his fingers. "I choose to kill, and I steal because it makes me feel powerful, gringo. Do not believe what Rip says about this gang having honor. There is no honor in what we are about to do."

"But the money is good?" Isiah questioned. "I mean, was he tellin' the truth about that?"

Sal grew silent. He hadn't seen more than a few hundred dollars each month since he broke out of jail last year. Rip had practically begged Salazar and Charles to come back to the gang with the promise of money beyond their wildest dreams. "The money goes to mi familia," he replied after a while. "We get a cut after each job, and they hold the rest in Reno with Rip's hermana, Beatrice."

"Why?"

"Rip trusts no one with the money except her. Besides, if the law comes knocking, they will have a hard time proving we robbed the stagecoaches," Sal explained with a shrug. "That is all I know."

"Seems odd."

"What does?"

"That you all just take his word for it," Isiah said. "What if… Well, what if there's no money in Reno?"

"The others trust him. Charles believes Rip will fulfill his promises."

"But not you? Don't you trust Rip?"

"I trust Charles," Sal stated firmly. "And only him."

"You two seem close."

"He does not see a worthless Mexican when he looks at me, but a man who is equal to him." Sal looked at Charles then. His friend had ridden to the crossroads to ensure the wagon came their way. "Charles saved my life."

"Why don't you follow Rip?" Isiah asked curiously.

"Because he is not the man he used to be. Our gang was once strong. Almost fifty of us. He has not been the same since the Royal Hearts killed the others. He is… distracted."

"But—"

"Enough questions." Salazar's dark eyes scanned across the landscape.

The tall grass in the valley obscured his vision. Sal rode ahead a few paces. He squinted against the sunlight and spotted a wagon near the fork in the road where Charles blocked the path to the city.

Sal pulled his mask onto the lower half of his face and gave the signal. Charles fired a single shot, spooking the horses and sending the wagon right toward Sal and the others.

Hector and Isiah rode side by side, coming up beside the wagon as it approached. Sal sat menacingly astride his horse. The driver reached for a gun, but Sal was quicker. The knife in his hand soared through the air and hit the man square in the shoulder with a sickening thwack.

Sal watched as the man tipped over and fell from the bench seat at the front of the wagon.

Sal slid from the saddle and came around the side of the wagon. "Destroy what is not valuable," he ordered. "And do not forget to leave our mark." His gloved hands tore open crates in search of treasures and trinkets. He tossed boxes of food out onto the road, dug through bags of fabric, carved open sacks of flour and sugar. Sal almost thought the job had gone sour until he found a strongbox hidden at the back of the wagon.

Sal pulled the strongbox outside and dropped it on the road. He stomped over to the driver and ripped his knife out of the man's shoulder before he kicked him for good measure. A chuckle burst from his lips as he made his way back to the strongbox. He jammed the blade into the lock until he heard it pop.

Banknotes, watches, fancy pens, and a few golden rings were tucked away inside of a small bag. Sal pocketed the money and tossed the rest to Hector. "Take it to the fence in Timber," he said. "And be back before the boss suspects anything. If he asks, just tell him the job went badly."

Hector hesitated. "Why are we keeping the money?"

"Split it between us," Sal replied. "The boss does not need to know."

Isiah came forward. He took the bag from Hector and said, "I'll do it."

Sal nodded. He gestured dismissively with his hand, and the gang left without him. A pained moan drew his attention back to the driver.

The man had crawled several feet in his absence. Sal pressed his boot to the center of the man's back. "Where do you think you are going?" he laughed. "I know you are hiding more money."

***

Timber, California

"There was an attack this morning," said Evan. "Out on Calligan Road."

Budd glanced up from his cup of coffee and nodded. He thought long and hard about what Evan had said. Calligan Road had once been safe for travel. Now it seemed as if Ripley Eagleson purposely targeted the road as some sort of message to Budd, a lesson in thinking he could outsmart the outlaw.

It would be foolish for Budd and the others to leave the inn. Still, there was a chance they could make it to the scene of the attack before the lawmen showed up. Budd stood up from his chair and dumped his coffee out the opened window.

He pulled on his coat and fetched Ivory from the public corral near the stables. Dawson stayed behind, but Evan and Blake joined him as he rode out of town toward Calligan Road.

A storm brewed overhead. Clouds moved swiftly toward the mountains as it began to rain. Budd turned his collar up to keep the chilly wind out. He shivered in the saddle, shifting uncomfortably.

The ride lasted until nightfall. A dark, angry sky stretched on for miles. Budd lit a lantern as they approached the wreckage up ahead. He gripped the reins tight and eased Ivory off the road. The worn leather beneath him groaned as he slid down from the saddle. There was mostly farmland along the outskirts of Sacramento. They had to be quick.

Rain trickled down the back of Budd's neck as he stood beside the overturned wagon. Water dripped from the tattered cover, soaking the wood of the wagon bed. Busted crates littered the road. Mashed apples, potatoes, berries, and other foods trailed alongside the hoof marks etched into the damp earth.

His eyes scanned the debris left in the attack's aftermath, searching for any sign that Ripley Eagleson's gang had been responsible.

Budd lifted his lantern and watched as the flickering light illuminated the inside of the wagon. There, partially hidden beneath chunks of timber, was an ace of spades pinned to the side of the wagon by a single throwing knife. It was the gang's signature—a signature that was sure to garner the wrong sort of attention from the marshal.

Budd crouched down and strained to reach the knife. His fingers brushed the handle as he groaned from the effort. The knife slid free. He pocketed the card and tucked the blade into his satchel for safe keeping.

"There's a partial trail leading back toward Timber, but the rain has muddled it all up. It'll be impossible to follow, even if one of us was a tracker," Evan told Budd. "What do we do now?"

"We leave this for the marshal to find, but we take the card with us. Let's not give Ripley Eagleson the satisfaction of using this attack to further his agenda." Budd lifted his lantern and took one long look at the scene before him.

It seemed as though a pack of wild beasts had descended upon the wagon and destroyed it with tooth and claw. The gang Ripley Eagleson was using for his wicked deeds had done away with whatever humanity and honor they had left. Budd was only grateful they hadn't happened upon any bodies.

He shut his eyes and tried to block out the horrible memories. Far too many of the attacks had ended in death. Budd remembered the first time he ever took a life, and it scarred him deeper than any wound ever could.

There were nights when he was haunted by the sight of John Pepper's last moments—haunted by the feeling he had when he pulled the trigger. Budd stared down at his hands and grimaced.

"Anything from Steven?" he asked Evan.

"He said Beatrice only leaves the house to send a handful of letters each week," his friend replied. "No sign of the gang in Reno. They got to be sticking around here for something big. It doesn't feel right."

Blake came around the wagon. He leaned against the wooden frame and scratched the back of his neck nervously. "They already destroyed half the city in the raid. Black Lake ain't nothin' more than a pile of black rubble. Think they might strike Sacramento again?"

Budd shook his head. "No," he answered. "The city is already weak. But maybe that's what he wanted. Maybe Ripley Eagleson wants Sacramento for himself. He just needs to leave the city isolated and vulnerable so he can take over."

"The only thing standing in his way is us," said Evan. "And that doesn't bode well."

Thunder rumbled, and the rain picked up. Budd grumbled under his breath and whistled for Ivory.

He hooked the lantern to the saddle and climbed onto the mare's back. Ivory's hooves sank into the shallow mud. She tossed her waterlogged mane and snickered.

"Easy, girl," Budd whispered to his mount.

Evan and Blake climbed onto their horses and followed Budd back toward Timber. Along the way, they kept their words to themselves. The sight of the destroyed wagon struck each man. They knew what had happened.

They knew the fear the driver must have felt. The terror. And that knowledge had kept their tongues from wagging until they reached town.

"Go on back to the room," Budd finally said. "I'll be back by sunrise... I just... need some time to think."

Budd looked around at Timber and felt a churning in his gut. The restlessness inside of his spirit matched the roiling storm that hovered over the town.

He was soaked to the bone and itching to get out of the rain. But Budd wasn't sure if the four walls of the room at the inn could withstand his emotions. Instead, he waved the others on and retreated to the stables, where he tended to his horse.

Chapter 4

The storm finally cleared the following morning. Marshal Greene and Ripley Eagleson stood beside a cot in the infirmary.

The merchant had been badly wounded and was on the brink of death when he crawled into town and claimed bandits had attacked his wagon. Just the sight of the man had caused a panic in the city. Rip almost smiled as he recalled the screams.

Though Rip had specifically told the gang to do the job quietly. Salazar's brutal creativity pleasantly surprised him. After all, the man had been barely recognizable, even after the doctor repaired most his injuries. There were thick bandages across the man's face, neck, and torso.

Rip rested his hand on the merchant's arm gently and gave it a reassuring squeeze. "We'll find the men responsible," he whispered. "Is there anything you can tell us about them?"

"Mexican... the man who did this to me was a Mexican. I could hear it in his voice," said the merchant. "He was in charge."

"Did he do or say anything you might remember?" asked the marshal.

"Two of the men discussed money. 'The boss doesn't need to know,' one of them said."

Red flashed through Rip's vision. He sucked in a harsh breath and struggled to rein in his control. His fists clenched tightly. His arms trembled from the effort it took not to bellow with rage.

The thought of his men being anything but loyal and obedient was unpleasant. How long had this betrayal been going on? How many of the bandits at the Old Mill had taken money from him? Questions whirled around in his mind until he caught sight of the marshal.

Marshal Greene gave Rip a questioning glance. His eyes flickered down to Rip's clenched fists before they returned to his face.

"You all right there, Eagleson?"

"Just furious these bandits could do something like this to an innocent man," he said. "It makes me weep for humanity."

"Just keep a cool head."

"Of course." Rip turned his attention back to the wounded merchant on the cot. "Is there anything else you remember?"

The merchant shook his head and grimaced. A pained expression came over the uncovered part of his face. It wasn't long before the man passed out from pain, or perhaps even the medicine the doctor had administered.

Rip followed Marshal Greene out of the infirmary and into the bright Sunday morning. The two of them then rode out to Calligan Road, where the attack had taken place.

Rip was in shock. He had told his men to rob the wagon, not to destroy the wagon. Even Marshal Greene cursed under his breath when he saw what remained of the merchant's things.

There was a profound sense of hatred surrounding the area that surprised Rip. For a moment, he wondered if he had pushed Salazar too far. The man was known for his cruelty, and Rip had taken advantage of their arrangement on several occasions.

But this act of rebellion wouldn't go unpunished. Not when everything Rip worked for was at stake.

He climbed down from his horse and toed open the empty strongbox. "Looks like they got what they were after," Rip said to the marshal. "There's no money or valuables left in here. Seems like Budd Mansfield and his gang have gotten desperate."

"I ain't too sure about that..."

Rip paused. He turned toward the marshal slowly and arched his right brow. "You don't think it's them? With all due respect, Marshal, I've seen what they're capable of."

"Where's the card?" Marshal Greene stood up from where he had been kneeling beside the wagon. He brushed his hands off onto his trousers and gestured around the scene. "There's no ace of spades in the wagon. Mr. Thayer's reports were adamant the gang left one behind after every attack."

"Perhaps they forgot it."

The marshal shook his head and sucked his teeth. "Nah, I very much doubt that. The gang has been careful so far. Why get messy now? Ain't like they got much to lose. And the witness said the man who attacked him was Mexican. Last I checked, Budd Mansfield wasn't Mexican."

"Well, we can't be certain." Rip pushed past the marshal and dropped to his knees beside the wagon. He searched high and low for the ace of spades. His hands brushed along the walls, feeling the cracks and splinters in the wood. The card was gone.

Someone had taken it, someone who knew Rip had been preparing for another attack. Budd Mansfield. Though Rip had ruined the man's reputation and made him a wanted criminal, Budd Mansfield was still only one step behind the gang.

Marshal Greene crouched down beside Rip. "This was a random attack. It could have been anyone. The roads are full of bandits these days."

Rip stood up with the marshal's help. He tidied his clothes and walked back toward his horse with his head hung low. But a strong hand wrapped itself around Rip's arm, halting his steps. It took all of his strength to keep from lashing out. He gritted his teeth and turned toward the marshal slowly. "Yes?"

"Why are you so sure it's Mansfield and his gang?" asked Marshal Greene as he dropped his hand. "There were only four bandits, and the leader was Mexican. That don't sound like the other attacks."

"I got a feeling in my gut that it's them. I can't shake it." Rip looked back at the wagon. "Let's ask around at the nearby farms. Maybe someone saw what happened."

But thundering hooves drew their gazes to the western road. A line deputy approached quickly. He pulled his horse to a stop just beside Rip and the marshal. "Pinkertons," the deputy panted. "They're here about Budd Mansfield."

Marshal Greene looked just as unhappy about Pinkerton's involvement as Rip felt. He should have known that Mansfield's former employers would catch wind of the attacks in Sacramento. Mansfield himself most likely contacted them.

***

Timber, California

Reno changed Steven Wright. Budd saw it in the man's gaze the second he walked into the room at the inn. There was a light there that hadn't existed a few months ago. In fact, Budd would have wagered all the money in his satchel that Steven had good news to share with them.

He moved across the room quickly and grabbed Steven, pulling him in for a brotherly hug. "Were you followed?" Budd asked. "God, it's good to see you."

"I was careful." Steven clapped Budd on the back before they separated. He then pulled a letter out of his coat pocket and handed it over. "I spoke with Beatrice. I know you said not to approach her, but I overheard a conversation she had with a servant, and I had to take a chance. We talked about what Ripley Eagleson's been up to."

Budd accepted the letter and opened it. "I don't understand. I thought Beatrice was involved in Eagleson's operation."

"She was," Steven said. "But losing Johnny changed things. Beatrice is willing to speak to Marshal Greene and a judge if you need her to."

There was doubt in Budd's mind, but he trusted Steven. Budd read through the letter and took his time as he tried to comprehend Beatrice's words. She explained how her suspicions had grown over the years where her brother was concerned and how Ripley had roped her into his lies.

Beatrice had defended Ripley and her late husband until the time had come when she couldn't handle it anymore. John Pepper's death had given Beatrice a fresh sight into what her brother was up to, things she described as treacherous. And now she wanted to help bring Ripley to justice.

It all seemed too good to be true. Perhaps it was just his own suspicious nature, but Budd wasn't yet convinced Beatrice was on their side. "I'll give it some thought," he promised Steven. "But this can't be the only news you've brought us."

The smile on Steven's face grew tenfold. He walked past Budd and took a seat beside his brother. "Hector Vasquez is in Timber," Steven said. "And he's headed back to the Old Mill tonight."

"How do you know?"

"I was in a shop before I came here. Hector didn't recognize me. Started talkin' to the owner of the shop, and I realized he was fencin' goods," explained Steven. "Figured he'd be takin' that money back to Rip if you wanted to follow him."

Budd got out his map and showed Steven the progress they've made toward finding a plan. Straying away from that plan was risky, but Budd's trust in Steven outweighed the doubts that ran through his mind.

He packed up his things and followed Steven out to the hitching post near the back entrance of the inn. Ivory waited patiently as a worker scraped mud from her horseshoes. Her ears twitched happily as Budd drew closer.

"Hey, girl." Budd patted Ivory's side and tossed the worker a few dollars for the trouble. He then hoisted himself into the saddle and rode with Steven to his camp near Yosemite Valley. The mountains were beautiful at that time of the year, but the two men were too lost in their thoughts to notice. They rode until day turned into night and the rain poured once more.

"It's just up here."

"You sure you don't want to wait for the others?" Budd asked. "Vasquez is slippery. He might run for it."

"They'll come tomorrow morning. Blake has some business to attend to at the quarry before your plan can work."

"The thought of your brother around explosives makes me uneasy," he admitted. "Blake ain't the most careful man I know. He has a tendency to get into trouble at the worst times."

Steven snorted, but he didn't argue. "How about Dawson? How's he takin' this?"

"He's worried about his new bride." Budd scratched at his stubbled chin. "He might not be willing to admit he played a role in all this, but I think he'll pull through when we need him to. Dawson is an honorable man. He'll do the right thing, even if it means breaking the law a few times. Justice is all that matters to us now."

"I don't know, Budd. You got more faith in him than I do."

"Evan says Dawson's a good man," Budd replied, and it was enough to convince Steven. After all, Evan was a hard man to impress despite his easygoing ways and wolfish grin. And if Evan accepted Dawson, then the others had no choice but to go along with it. "How far?"

"We're here." Steven hopped down from the saddle and grabbed a bag from beneath some underbrush. He opened the bag and tossed some clothing to Budd. "Put those on. Hector might not recognize me, but he'll know your face immediately. We dress as highwaymen and take him before he reaches the valley."

"Sounds simple enough," Budd scoffed. He swapped out his coat and hat before tying a bandana around his mouth and nose.

Steven smeared dirt across his neck and forehead before dabbing some on their clothes. "Ain't goin' to fool anybody into thinkin' you're a highwayman if you look freshly bathed," Steven chuckled. Once everything was in place, they took up posts along the main road leading into Yosemite Valley and waited. They waited until it grew too dark to see and the rain had soaked into their clothes. And they waited until a lantern flickered in the distance and the sound of hooves met their ears.

Hector Vasquez passed by Steven's post and moved toward Budd. Budd whistled and moved to the center of the road. He lifted his gun and cocked the hammer.

Fear entered the outlaw's gaze, and he dropped the lantern. It hit a rock, and the glass shattered upon impact, dousing the light.

"Get down from the horse," Budd growled. "Slowly."

Chapter 5

Lightning illuminated the dark corners of the eatery. Rip walked beside Marshal Greene as they entered the small building situated beside the hotel. Rip took a seat at the table where the server indicated.

The other men at the table wore simple suits, but their behavior marked them as outsiders. City folk from the east carried a stench of self-righteousness that turned Rip's stomach.

"Evening, gentlemen," Marshal Greene said as he sat beside Rip. "I don't believe we've met. I'm U.S. Marshal Eddison Greene."

"We know who you are," replied the first man. "And we know who Mr. Eagleson is... or is it Reginald Pearce?"

"You have us at a disadvantage, Mister...?"

"Jack Graham, and this is my partner, Lucas Smith," answered the first man.

Pinkertons were bad news. And Rip sat across from the two of them.

Graham and Smith quietly stirred their coffee as they flipped through several documents. Graham slid a contract across the table. It was a contract that Richard Hunt, the manager of Pratt & Dempcy's office in Reno, and Howard Thayer had signed.

"Let us not waste any of your time," said Smith. "We are all on the same side. The side of justice. And we want to make sure everything is in order before we send a man to the gallows."

"Budd Mansfield is as guilty as they come," Rip said.

Graham and Smith looked unconvinced.

Smith cleared his throat and said, "We just have a few questions for you, Mr. Eagleson."

"Questions?"

"You were once an employee of Pratt and Dempcy, weren't you?" asked Smith.

Rip nodded firmly. "There was a misunderstanding."

Smith glanced down at the papers in front of him and said, "You stole money from the stagecoach company. Howard Thayer caught you red-handed."

"I had my reasons. It was a mistake made in my youth, one that I regret every day," replied Rip. "What does this have to do with Budd Mansfield?"

"Unlike you, Mr. Eagleson, Budd Mansfield has no reason to target Pratt and Dempcy," Graham said as Smith wrote notes in a small journal.

Rip looked between the two men. Neither of their expressions gave away what they were thinking. Rip wanted to know what was behind their emotionless eyes. He had a hard time reading them, and that frightened him. There was no way of telling if they were on Mansfield's side or not.

"Budd Mansfield used to work for us. I hired him myself." Jack Graham crossed his arms over his chest. He leaned back in his seat and pinned Rip with an inquisitive stare that made him squirm in his seat a little. "I've known Budd Mansfield for over ten years. Never once did I question his honor."

"People change." Rip matched the detective's posture. The material of his suit stretched tight over his shoulders as he crossed his arms. "Budd Mansfield killed those people. He killed my brother-in-law, and he killed what hope I had left."

"He fought against a band of outlaws who attacked Sacramento and Black Lake. He also stayed behind for weeks to help rebuild Sacramento and looked for survivors in Black Lake after they put the fires out," argued Graham. "What sort of criminal does that, Mr. Eagleson?"

"I'm not sure. Between the two of us, you are the expert," Rip retorted. "I'm merely a victim of Budd Mansfield's crimes. I don't know how the man thinks." Rip wasn't sure how things worked in Chicago, but he very much disliked someone disregarding his reputation.

He was a well-respected citizen of Sacramento, and he refused to back down. Anyone in the city would have told the Pinkertons that Ripley Eagleson was incapable of harming a fly.

"Whoever is responsible will be punished to the full extent of the law," Smith said. "So, for your sake, let's hope you are telling the truth."

The two Pinkertons stood up from the table and left the eatery. Marshal Greene exhaled a long breath and finally relaxed in his seat. Rip, however, remained tense. He felt as if there was someone watching him from the shadows. The hair on the back of his neck stood up.

Salazar.

"Let me know if anything changes," Rip said to Marshal Greene as he stood up to leave.

He exited through the back door and nearly ran right into Sal—who was still swathed from head to toe in the dark clothes he wore during the attack. Rip grabbed Sal by his injured arm and dragged him beneath the staircase behind the eatery.

"I ought to kill you dead," Rip hissed. He smacked Sal on the head and shoved him against the wall of the eatery. "Stealing from me! You didn't think I would find out?"

Sal pushed off the wall and lunged at Rip. The two men fell to the ground, and a hand wrapped around Rip's throat. He swallowed against a calloused palm and stilled.

Sal's angry face glared down at him. It would have been so easy, so simple, of a thing for Salazar to kill Rip just then. But he stayed his hand. The threat remained, nonetheless. A heated mark upon Rip's neck where Sal's hand had been.

Rip trembled at the mere thought of Salazar's strength, let alone his prowess for killing. He sucked in a harsh breath when he was released. His face was bright red with shame and embarrassment. How had things gotten so far outside of his control? "Whether or not you like it, Salazar, you owe me your loyalty."

"I owe you my life. Not my loyalty," Sal said as he turned to leave, but Rip stopped him.

"Fine, have it your way," he spat. "You left a witness alive. Take care of it. Consider this an act of servitude and nothing more. And seeing as you are my servant and you saw fit to steal from me, I'll be keeping your cut of the fenced goods."

***

Timber, California

It was a day's ride back to Timber. Budd came into town about an hour before sunrise. He left Ivory at the stables and walked down to the saloon, pushing his way through the doors. The owner gave him the usual speech about not causing trouble as he passed. Several patrons gawked openly, but none of them dared approach.

None except Jack Graham, who embraced Budd the moment he came to a stop beside the table. "You're in a world of trouble, my friend," Graham whispered. "Ripley Eagleson and Mayor Thomas are pushing for a hanging."

Budd took a step back and removed his hat before taking a seat. "Ripley Eagleson would shoot me himself if given the chance." He ordered a pair of beers with just a gesture, and the saloon girl fetched their drinks.

Ginger gave Budd a worried glance, but he smiled reassuringly. She set the bottles on the table and scurried off to serve the others in the saloon.

"Did you meet with Rose and Douglas?" Budd asked his old friend.

"Rose refused to see me, but I spoke with Douglas when I arrived in Sacramento." Graham looked around nervously. "He seems to believe the papers."

"He always was a gullible fool." Budd bounced his leg beneath the table, feeling a swell of unease between them as they sat in silence. He scrapped the pleasantries and got to the point. "Why are you here, Jack? I asked you to come to Sacramento last year, and you denied my letters."

"I heard you were in Timber a few days ago, and I needed to reach out the only way I knew how. Glad you still use the same false name as the one in Chicago. It was easier to send a telegram than to meet in person."

"So why meet now?" Budd asked. He wasn't sure why his old friend had come all the way to California, but he was certain it wasn't good. "You could have sent word. Even a rejection letter would have been better than hearing nothing at all."

"Mr. Thayer and his associates have decided they want the agency to look into the matters surrounding your arrest," Graham told Budd. "I was requested."

"Why do I sense you ain't telling me everything?"

"Because they requested Lucas to accompany me," said Graham.

Budd shook his head and cursed under his breath. Last thing he needed was for his past to catch up with him while he dealt with the Ripley Eagleson situation. His contract with the Pinkerton detective agency had ended because he hadn't seen eye to eye with Lucas Smith.

The man had it out for Budd almost as bad as Ripley Eagleson. His presence in Sacramento was another hitch in Budd's plans.

"I don't need this right now, Jack. Does he believe the rumors, or are you keeping him wise?" Budd asked.

"Lucas will do his job so long as he knows I'm watching him."

But that didn't provide any comfort to Budd. "That ain't a real answer, Graham. And you know it. He'll try to bury me before the doctor even declares I'm a dead man."

"No one is dying, all right," Graham grumbled. "I need you to trust me on this, Budd. I'm on your side. I just don't know which side the marshal is on. He seems like a good enough man, but he was quick to mark you as guilty."

"Think he might buy into what Ripley Eagleson is saying?"

"I don't know," Graham answered honestly. "But I know you need no more enemies than you've got around here. Just keep your head down and let me handle it."

Budd shook his head once more. "Not when I've got a shot at making this right. I'm sorry, Jack, but I'm too close to ending this to walk away now."

"Close to what?"

"There is a ledger," said Budd. "A ledger proving that Ripley Eagleson was doing all the crimes and not me. And his sister Beatrice will testify on my behalf."

Graham looked nervous. "Stay away from Eagleson and his sister."

"I can't do that."

The Pinkerton detective slammed his palm on the table. The beers rattled, and several heads turned in their direction. Graham leaned closer and lowered his voice to a deep rumble. "You need to learn where to draw the line, Budd. You take too many risks. That's why you ended up in a jail cell. Now, do as I say and keep your head down."

Budd couldn't promise what Graham needed him to. "He took more than my good name. He took my honor. Hell, I barely know who I am anymore, Jack. I need this more than you could ever know. Too much of me is tied up in catching Eagleson."

"If he really is responsible for everything they accused you of, you need to be careful," Graham sighed. "I hate the thought of losing a good friend to a cold-blooded killer."

"It's Eagleson who needs to be careful. He'll mess up, I know it. I'm too close for his comfort, and it's making him desperate." Budd downed the last of his beer and headed outside.

His boots hit the sidewalk just beyond the door, and he glanced down the road in search of unseen enemies. He eased out onto the street, taking his time as he made his way back to the stables. Jack Graham wouldn't risk reaching out again, not when Budd had stated his intentions. The lines had been drawn, despite what Graham thought.

Budd was squarely on one side, and Ripley Eagleson was on the other. There was no way this ended with both of them alive and free. Either Budd proved his innocence and took Eagleson down, or Eagleson won and Budd lived the rest of his days as a wanted man.

Chapter 6

Salazar came around the corner just as the nurse locked up the physician's office for the night. He watched her closely, waiting for the opportune moment. Once she was out of sight, he moved to the back of the building. Sal almost tumbled out of the saddle, but he caught himself on the saddle horn.

Pain lanced up his arm and shoulder. Sal grunted. Sweat poured down his face as he tried to control his breathing. He slowly lowered himself to the ground. His head spun for a moment, but he quickly stumbled over to the building.

The shutters on the window opened quietly. Sal lifted himself up with one arm and climbed through. He stepped carefully across the floor and stopped beside a cot in the corner.

The merchant seemed to have slept restlessly, a cold sweat beaded on his upper lip and brow. It was as if the man sensed his end was near.

With one swift yank, he tugged the pillow from beneath the merchant's head and slammed it over his gasping face. Arms and legs wiggled wildly as the merchant fought to stay alive. But Sal doubled his efforts. Nails scraped down his forearm. Fingers dug into the muscles of his biceps. Legs kicked and squirmed, bucking like a wild horse.

Salazar watched as the man's eyes rolled into the back of his skull. The body went limp on the cot, and he slowly released the pressure. It sickened the bloodthirsty beast inside him, the part of him that preferred a messier end for his victims.

But the boss demanded the merchant go quietly into the night. Sal wished he had given the man a more honorable death. After all, he had fought with a hunger for life that Sal envied. The scrapes and nail marks on his arms were a testament to that hunger.

Sal dropped the pillow onto the floor and shuffled over to a cabinet along the wall. He took several bottles of medicine and stuffed them into his pockets, along with some fresh bandages. Sal then left through the window. He hit the ground with a quiet thud. His horse nudged his arm and Sal hissed.

The knife wound had grown infected. Sweat and dirt discolored the bandage. He tucked his arm against his side as he pulled himself into the saddle.

Charles waited near the edge of town, munching on an apple without a care in the world. He tossed the core to the ground and waved Sal down. "Any sign of Hector in the city?"

"No," Sal answered. "Not for days now."

"That ain't good, partner."

"Do you think he ran for it?" he asked. Sometimes Salazar had contemplated doing something similar. "The border, I mean."

"Ain't no border goin' to protect him from Rip's wrath if he did. No, my guess is Mansfield bein' alive out there got to him and he spooked."

"Whether or not he left, it makes no difference to me." Sal pulled a cigarette from his satchel and lit the end with a match. Bitter smoke filled his lungs and left the taste of tobacco on his tongue. "We need to head back to the Old Mill. Transport is Wednesday morning."

"It'll take three days to get back with that arm of yours," Charles said as he reached over and peeled back the bandage on Salazar's arm. He grimaced. "Might have to close that thing with a hot iron before we go."

"If you burn me, I will shoot you."

Laughter exploded from Charles. "What do you think happened to Hector?"

"I think he drank too much and is now regretting it."

"What about the money from the fenced goods?"

Sal shrugged. "We will never know for sure. Besides, fewer men in the gang means more money for us, sí?" Sal grinned as he rode beside his closest friend.

They trekked back to the Old Mill and made it just in time to catch the wagon before it left. Three bandits from Isiah's camp were dressed in average clothes, ready to guard the wagon on its journey to Reno. Rip was nowhere to be seen. Sal eased himself down from the horse and walked into the building.

Papers were scattered as far as the eye could see. Rip stood in the middle of the room with a scowl on his face. "Beatrice has betrayed me," Rip announced in a strange and hollow voice. "She sent a messenger with a letter. It says she no longer wishes to watch over the money, that she cannot bear to support my wicked deeds any longer." Rip tore up the paper in his hand and snapped his fingers.

His personal servant rushed inside and cleaned the mess on the floor.

"What about the transport?" Sal asked, though he sensed there was more to the story than Rip had told him. "The money is safe?"

"Yes, I'm sending someone to the estate in Reno. They'll look after the money in Beatrice's stead." Rip closed his eyes and took several deep breaths. He then walked over to Sal. "Hector is missing."

"Sí."

"When did you see him last?" Rip asked. "Did he seem… different?"

"Hector was fine. Charles thinks it is Budd Mansfield who took him." Salazar circled Rip. Suspicion dripped from his voice as he said, "It is no secret he is the one who is watching our every move. He is like a wolf who has caught the scent of his prey."

"We will deal with Budd Mansfield with. We simply need to be patient." Rip smiled, but the corners of his mouth twitched. He had lied so many times that Salazar knew the signs. Rip was afraid of Budd Mansfield.

"What has the mayor said about a new sheriff? I don't want to deal with any lawmen like Dawson." Sal leaned against the wall and cleaned his nails with his knife.

"Isiah's man is ready for when Mayor Thomas sets a date for the election."

***

En Route to Reno, Nevada

The watch in his hand ticked quietly. Budd checked the time once more. Quarter after noon. Right on time. His gaze roamed over the road. Ivory trembled with excitement. The wagon appeared, rattling as it came into view. He tucked his watch into his satchel and unholstered his gun. Budd and Ivory made their way to the center of the road.

"I told you the truth. Now let me go," Hector Vasquez demanded.

"You ain't going anywhere," Budd replied. "It'll snow in hell before I let another outlaw go free, Vasquez. Might as well be grateful I'm keeping you alive."

"When my boss finds out you have me—"

Evan kicked the outlaw, knocking him unconscious where he sat hogtied against the rocks. "I've heard enough out of him. Let's get into position. This will be a fight."

Budd nodded and gripped the reins tighter. He waited impatiently, pacing Ivory across the road until the wagon stopped.

Two men jumped out of the back with guns. A third armed man rode up front with the driver. Evan, Blake, and Steven surrounded the wagon. Budd rode up beside the wagon and approached the driver.

"Surrender," he ordered. "Or things will get ugly real fast."

"I don't think I will." The driver's hideously scarred face twisted up into a gruesome smile. A gunshot rang in the valley. Budd leaped from the back of his horse. He landed on his side, climbed to his feet, smacked Ivory on the rear, and sent the horse running off to safety. Evan returned fire. The wagon lurched forward and nearly ran Budd down.

Budd jumped out of the way at the last second. He gave chase the moment his shock had worn off. Boots pounded upon the dirt road as he caught up.

His fingers flexed, stretching toward the wagon as he picked up the pace. Budd took a leap of faith and smacked into the side of the wagon. His hands scrambled for purchase, nails scraping across the wood. He grabbed onto the wall of the wagon bed and pulled himself up.

Bullets whizzed past his head as he climbed up. Sunlight spilled in through the holes that appeared on the cover. Budd rolled to avoid getting shot.

Large crates slid from side to side in the back of the wagon, nearly crushing Budd as he stopped to catch his breath. He braced his legs against the wall and stopped a crate before it got any further.

Budd panted heavily, gasping for air. His lungs burned. He gripped the edge of the crate and lifted himself up. The lid opened as the wagon turned the corner. Fine jewelry, pocket watches, exquisite fabrics, and expensive baubles filled the crate.

Budd popped open the other lids and whistled. It was filled with money. Another held large rocks. Upon closer inspection, Budd realized that there were flecks of gold peeking out of the rocks. There was a small fortune in the wagon.

He closed the lids and climbed toward the front. The driver laughed as he barreled down the road. Budd used his knife and sliced open the wagon cover. He grabbed onto the reins and pulled back hard, forcing the wagon to a sudden stop. Budd fell into the driver.

"I told you to surrender!"

"You ain't no lawman!" shouted the bandit. The ink on his forearm marked him as a criminal, but even if he worked for Eagleson, he wasn't part of the Blood Eagle Gang.

Budd smashed his fist into the bandit's jaw and knocked him off the wagon. The bandit recovered quickly. He spat blood into the dirt and gestured for Budd to come closer.

Budd circled the man, watching for any sign of weakness. His fist ached, but he landed another punch to the bandit's middle. "Who do you work for?" he asked as the man dropped to his knees. "Answer me or this gets worse for you."

"Isiah West!"

"Since when does West do business with Ripley Eagleson?" Budd questioned. He had heard of Isiah before, seen his picture on wanted posters all over Reno. "Last I checked, he was in Mexico looking for a way to the Caribbean."

The bandit shook his head and snorted. "Isiah got a letter from Eagleson back when Pratt and Dempcy owned these roads. Hell, every bandit outfit in the region got one. Said he was workin' on somethin' big and needed as many men as we could spare. The boss supposed it was high time he got somethin' to show for all his hard work."

Budd jumped back as a fist came flying toward his face. The bandit crawled to his feet. They danced around each other, waiting for the opportune time to strike. Budd evaded an attack and kicked the bandit back. "What's Eagleson promising these bandits?"

"Money."

"And?" Budd prodded. He kept the bandit talking, kept him distracted as Evan moved into position. "If money was all he promised, you lot could have robbed the stagecoaches yourselves. Why work for a man like Ripley?"

"Power. Towns like Black Lake cross Ripley Eagleson and burn for it. But Timber," the man drawled. "Timber is a shinin' example of what could happen if an outlaw runs things."

"He wants Sacramento…"

"He wants the whole dang territory," said the bandit. "If you hadn't gotten in the way, he would have succeeded by now! If he had—"

Budd gave the signal.

Evan tackled the bandit to the ground and wrenched his arms behind his back. Budd helped his partner hogtie the rest of the outlaws while Blake and Steven stood guard.

They loaded the bandits and the loot up into the wagon and rode to Sacramento under the cover of nightfall. The city was quiet when they arrived, but Budd kept his head down. Once the wagon was secure, he wrote a letter to Marshal Greene and pinned it to the frame.

Chapter 7

Beatrice had betrayed him. His lovely sister had somehow found the strength to defy him. Her disobedience was unforgivable.

Rip was distraught over Beatrice's decision to help Budd Mansfield. He paced the floor of his room at the hotel well into the late hours of the night. He paced until a restless sleep claimed him, and even then he couldn't find peace. Dreams of shackles and a swinging noose invaded his mind and held him hostage.

Rip tossed and turned, tangling the linens around his legs. Sweat dampened his shirt and the pillow beneath his head. The sound of his own grinding teeth filled the room and echoed down the corridor of the hotel.

A sharp knock on the door startled Rip awake. He blinked open his eyes and slid his legs out of the bed. Bare feet slapped upon the wooden floorboards as he crept across the room.

Rip cracked open the door and was greeted by the sight of two Pinkertons. Jack Graham and Lucas Smith stood on the other side of the door.

"How can I help you, gentlemen?" Rip grumbled sleepily. He opened the door wider and allowed them into his room.

"We still have a few questions to ask you."

"And what would those questions be?" Rip feigned calmness as he lit the remnants of his cigar and took a long drag. Smoke floated out of his nostrils. He gestured for the Pinkertons to take a seat, but they declined. Instead, they crowded around Rip as he went about his morning routine.

"Where were you last Friday evening?" Smith asked.

"I was here."

"So, you are unaware that Mr. Lowe is dead?"

Rip's forehead crinkled in confusion. "Who?"

"The merchant," Graham snapped. "The man who you promised justice."

Rip nodded as he continued to pretend, as though he was unfazed by the two men who stood in his room. "My condolences to his family. Death is never easy."

"Aren't you going to ask how he died?" Graham took a step toward Rip, but Smith held him back. Still, the agent was livid. "Someone smothered him with his own pillow," Graham spat vehemently. "A man was seen leaving through a window only moments before the body was discovered. The killer does not match Budd Mansfield's description."

"Perhaps he had enemies?" Rip said. He stared the Pinkerton detective in the eyes. Never once had he allowed his facade to crack. "Why are you telling me this?"

"Because as of dawn, you are on our list of suspicious persons," Smith answered.

"Me? How could you suspect me?"

"Why don't you get dressed and come with us," Graham suggested. "It will be easier to show you rather than have us explain it."

Rip didn't like the sound of that. He dressed quickly and met the two agents outside the sheriff's office. Several deputies surrounded what looked like a bullet-riddled wagon, and Rip's heart skipped.

He paused, taking in the sight of his loot being carried out of the wagon by lawmen. Mayor Thomas and Marshal Greene stood side by side, holding a small note between them. Marshal Greene spotted Rip in the crowd and waved him over.

Rip greeted the lawman with a tip of his hat and cleared his throat. "Good morning, Marshal, Mayor" he said. "What seems to be the problem here?"

"No problem at all, actually." Marshal Greene handed Rip the note.

Thought you might like these back. —Budd Mansfield

It was a simple note, but those few scrawled words on a scrap of paper nearly sent Rip into a fit of hysterics. His face grew white as a sheet, and he felt sick to his stomach.

Budd Mansfield had intercepted his delivery and brought the stolen goods right to the marshal's doorstep. Just that small gesture had created doubt in everyone's minds where Ripley Eagleson was concerned.

After all, how many outlaws would have returned the items they stole? None, thought Rip—which must have been why the marshal eyed him suspiciously.

"Is Mansfield known for doing this?" asked Marshal Greene.

Mayor Thomas shook his head. "I've never seen something like this before. It looks like everything from the last two robberies has been returned…"

Rip felt as though all his hard work had quickly become unraveled. He grabbed the mayor by the arm and steered him off to the side. "Do not let yourself fall victim to his lies," Rip told Mayor Thomas. "Budd Mansfield manipulated Howard Thayer for years. Now look where we are. He's playing a game, Mr. Mayor, and he's playing to win."

"Are you sure?"

"I know John wasn't a good man, but he was my brother," Rip whimpered. He felt his eyes burn from well-practiced tears. "And Mansfield killed him. I saw it with my own two eyes, and then he threatened to kill me too if I came forward. He's a wicked, evil man."

"I trust you, Eagleson," the mayor replied. "We will keep on the hunt for Mansfield. I won't stop until he's brought to justice."

Rip shook the mayor's hand and dabbed the corners of his eyes with a handkerchief. He then sauntered into the sheriff's office, where Isiah West's captured men sat, locked in a cell. The man who had been driving the wagon looked up at Rip expectantly.

"Ain't you goin' to get us out of here?" asked the bandit.

Rip brought his arm up, grabbed the man by the jaw, and yanked him so hard against the bars that they nearly knocked him unconscious. "You will not speak a word to anyone," Rip whispered harshly. "You will wait out your time behind these bars like a good chap, and then we will fetch you when I say so. Until then, you best do the intelligent thing and keep your mouth closed."

The bandit fell backward as Rip released his grip. It was almost comical watching as the hardened criminal scampered away on his hands and knees. If not for the ever-present issue of Budd Mansfield looming over his head, Rip might have even cracked a smile.

***

The Old Mill

Isiah panted heavily, trying his best to crawl across the floor. No one helped him. No one stopped Salazar when he brought his boot down upon his head over and over.

Sal roared with fury. He hated outsiders. He hated there was a camp of spineless bandits so close to where he slept. But most of all, he hated that Isiah's men had gotten captured by Budd Mansfield so easily. They were pathetic. All of them. And so Sal had dragged Isiah out to the camp and made an example out of him.

"Get up!" Sal barked. "On your feet! Face me like a real man."

Isiah spat blood onto the ground and stood up on wobbly legs. "Stop this madness…"

"Stop? You want me to stop?" Sal chuckled. "I thought you wanted to be one of us. I thought you wanted to impress the boss with all of your tricks, gringo. Now you beg at my feet like a wounded dog looking for scraps to eat."

"It weren't my fault they got caught!"

Sal hit Isiah so hard that it sounded like a gunshot echoing in a canyon. His fist bashed into the underside of Isiah's jaw and sent the large bandit leader sprawling to the ground once again. "A leader takes responsibility for his men," he said. "And he pays for their mistakes with blood. This is our way."

To Sal's surprise, Isiah laughed. He rolled onto his side and cackled like a madman. "Rip has you all wrapped around his finger, don't he?" Isiah snorted. "You said you didn't trust him, that there weren't no honor in this gang, but you're just as foolish as the rest of Sacramento. Ripley Eagleson ain't no one's savior!" Isiah slowly climbed back to his feet. He swayed from left to right, unable to balance himself properly.

Sal disliked that the bandit leader had seen through him so easily. Perhaps there was a part of him that had hoped Charles had been right about Rip, right that their boss had fought for them as hard as they worked for him.

Each time they headed out on the road to attack another stagecoach, was another risk to their lives. And Rip didn't seem to care. In fact, Sal couldn't remember the last time they heard words of praise that weren't followed by a punch to the gut or a bullet to the leg.

But he remembered the times when all they had was each other, and that kept Sal from walking away. The Blood Eagles had been his family when no one else had given him a chance. His sister deserved a good life. She deserved the money he made robbing the rich folks who rode in Pratt & Dempcy stagecoaches. And Rip had promised there was only one job left—a job that could change their lives.

"So long as you are on his land, he is your savior," Salazar replied. "And you would do well not to anger him."

"Or what?" Isiah hissed. "Or I'll go missin' like Hector and Leroy? Or will I end up dead like John and Pete?"

Sal shrugged as if he couldn't care less. "He will tell me to kill you, and I will enjoy taking your life."

"Obey or die. That's it?" Isiah shoved against Salazar's chest.

Charles stepped forward, looking as though he wanted to defend Sal, but Sal shook his head. Sal wasn't like Rip. He was not the sort of man who allowed others to fight his battles.

Sal dropped his hand to his belt. His fingers grazed the handle of his knife, but he grabbed his gun instead.

"Salazar!" Rip's voice boomed in the camp. "He will work to make up for his mistake. Stand down."

Sal's hand trembled as he fought the urge to pull the trigger. He lowered the gun and took several deep breaths to calm himself. His gaze turned to Rip. Everything in him screamed out in defiance. He felt nothing for the man who claimed to be his brother, his superior.

"Saddle up," Rip ordered. "Isiah, Salazar, Charles, and Dwight ride with me. The rest of you get back to work. We need to be ready to take the city in one week."

Dwight Cobb looked less than enthused about joining the gang on a raid. The outlaw seemed downright angry that he had been chosen to follow Rip after all Isiah had said. It seemed whatever spell Rip had woven around folks had finally worn off.

The outlaws had once seen Ripley Eagleson as their king. Now, people saw Rip the way Salazar had always seen him. As nothing more than a swindler. Still, there was money to be made. Money Sal could use to get one step further from Ripley Eagleson's influence.

They saddled up and rode along the path that wound through the mountains. It took them further north than

Sacramento to where the forests were denser and there were fewer settlements.

"What are we doing all the way out here?" Sal asked Rip as they set up camp for the night.

"There's a homestead being built a few miles west from here," Rip explained. "And the last of Pratt and Dempcy's stagecoaches in California are transporting the new landowners to their humble beginnings. They will carry everything they own."

It sounded like a good payday. "But what is the catch? You would not have brought Isiah and Dwight if you were not expecting trouble." Sal laid out his bedroll beside the fire and warmed himself as he awaited Rip's answer.

Rip said, "There is a chance Budd Mansfield has also heard about the transport."

"And you're just tellin' us now?" Dwight cursed.

Salazar unholstered his gun and held it up toward the light of the crackling fire. "If Budd Mansfield shows his face on that road, I will shoot him myself."

Chapter 8

The Old Mill

The wind rustled through the trees. Budd stood on the cliff overlooking the Old Mill. He had watched as outlaws strolled around the courtyard, tended to horses, and camped along the outer perimeter of the building. An enormous wall of timbers surrounded the Old Mill, and the front gate was constantly manned by armed guards.

Budd heard a twig snap behind him and glanced over his shoulder at Dawson. "I ain't trying to argue with you today," he said with a weary sigh. "We set the plan in place, and we're going through with this whether or not you come along."

"We can't just let them rob that stagecoach."

"They are three days ahead of us, and we only have this one chance to get it right," Budd replied. "Evan is already moving into position on the western side of the bandit camp."

Dawson shook his head and pointed to the wall that surrounded the Old Mill. "You will get us all killed trying to take that fort."

"We ain't taking it," he said for what felt like the hundredth time that morning. "We're getting inside just long enough to find the ledger, and then we are coming right back here before Rip and the gang return."

They had only a small window of opportunity. Everything had to go as planned, or else Budd was doomed. He scrubbed a hand over his face and tucked his binoculars into his satchel.

"You don't have to trust me," Budd told Dawson. "You don't even have to like me. But you have to make a choice. I ain't going to keep protecting you out here. Either you're with us or you're not."

Dawson lowered his head. He mindlessly shuffled his feet and gazed out at the horizon. There was fear and doubt surrounding him, wafting like a foul odor.

"I'm not meant for this life. I can't stand by and risk doing this when I know people are in danger. I'm a lawman, Budd. And I'm going after that stagecoach."

Budd turned around and offered his hand. "I can't say I'm not disappointed, but I suppose I understand. Sometimes justice is found outside the law, and that don't sit right with everybody. Good luck."

"Goodbye, Budd Mansfield, and good luck to you." Dawson shook Budd's hand and picked his bag up from the camp. The former lawman strapped his bag to the saddle and climbed onto his horse. He rode off in the direction Ripley Eagleson and his gang had traveled, hoping to stop the robbery.

Once Dawson disappeared into the forest, Budd met with Blake and Steven Wright. The two brothers kept Hector Vasquez tied to a nearby tree with a scarf tied between his teeth to keep the outlaw from making too much noise.

They sipped their morning coffee casually. Blake smiled at Budd as he drew nearer, while Steven gave him a quick nod of acknowledgement.

"Saw Dawson leave," Blake muttered between gulps. "Evan won't be happy. He was hoping Dawson would've come to his senses by now."

"Maybe Dawson is the only one of us who has come to his senses," Budd chuckled. "If you had told me a month ago that I'd be a wanted man about to break into the most protected fort in the region, I might have called you a madman."

"Lord knows I've been called worse," Steven said.

They cleaned up camp and left the horses behind. It was a half day's journey on foot from the cliffs to the trail leading to the Old Mill. Budd pulled out his map and followed the way to the hidden entrance that Pete had told them about.

The opening was just wide enough for two horses and a wagon to fit through, which was how the gang had been transporting the loot. Budd spotted the gate up ahead, as well as the two guards.

"Where's Evan?" Blake whispered. "There's too many of them in the courtyard."

Just then, an explosion echoed through the valley. Bandits got onto their horses and dashed off in the smoke's direction.

Budd put the map away and rushed the two guards at the gate. In the chaos, they hadn't seen him coming. He knocked the first one out and wrapped his arm around the second guard's neck before he could scream for help. Steven and Blake got the gate open just as the bandit camp cleared out.

Budd dragged the guard inside and choked him until he was unconscious. The guard slumped to the ground quietly.

Budd led the others over to a large timber door. He pulled the handle up and yanked it open. It squeaked loudly, but the sound was covered by a second explosion. Steven and Blake lifted their guns and entered the building. Budd covered the rear with his rifle. They moved swiftly and quietly, listening for any signs of life inside.

"Check the back room," he said. "Pete told Dotty that's where they kept the loot."

Steven moved over to the second door and pushed it open. It was filled with crates similar to what had been in the back of the transport wagon. "No one is here," he told Budd. "We're good."

Budd took a moment and stared around the large space. The space was empty aside from a single table and six chairs. Budd ran his hand along the edge of the table, looking for hidden compartments or drawers where Ripley Eagleson might have hidden the ledger. He searched the chairs and the floor but came up empty handed.

"Over here," Blake called.

In front of him, at the back of the loot room, was a safe.

***

Sacramento, California

Rip opened his eyes at the sight of a dreary gray sky. He huffed and sat upright, taking in the world around him before he finally stood up.

The men snored loudly in their bedrolls. Rip kicked Salazar's boots, startling the man awake. He stretched above his head and ordered, "Get ready. We leave in fifteen minutes."

Sal grumbled under his breath as he awakened. The outlaw walked around the camp and got everyone up and moving. They packed up the camp and stored a cache in a tree, just in case. After that, the gang saddled up and rode north along the forest's edge. There was a road that connected Sacramento to a newer settlement.

Rip positioned the gang upon a hillside. He pulled on his mask and watched the road. "Mr. Cobb," Rip said. "It would be in your best interest to follow Salazar's lead and keep your mouth closed."

"What about the rest of us?" asked Isiah West. The bandit leader was already on Rip's bad side after the mess he made of the last job. Rip disliked incompetent leaders almost as much as he disliked lawmen.

"Stay out of my way and do as I tell you," Rip stated plainly. "Another mishap, like the transport I put you in charge of, and I'll be having your head. Got that?"

Before Isiah replied, there was a great shout of alarm. Rip's head whipped around and his gaze landed on the stagecoach. The conversation had distracted him. He bellowed with anger, the sound partially muffled by his mask, and rode hard after the stagecoach as it barreled past them.

A gust of wind kicked up dirt and rocks as the stagecoach soared down the road. Storm's hooves beat a furious rhythm as Rip tried to catch up with the coach.

He spurred on his horse, urging the enormous beast on. Storm gave a great big lunge and surged to the front of the stagecoach. Rip cocked his revolver and shot the driver.

The stagecoach veered off the road and hit a steep embankment. It rolled down the hillside, hitting several trees before it came to a sudden halt beside the river.

Rip pulled his mask down and whistled for his men. Salazar led the way to the stagecoach, weaving between the trees until he came upon the wreckage.

"Only two passengers," he shouted up to Rip. "No guards."

Rip steered Storm down the embankment and toward the ravine.

They forced a woman with fire red hair and porcelain skin out of the stagecoach and shoved her to her knees. Her hands sank into the mud, and she wept openly. Vivid green eyes looked up at Rip as he approached. "Will you kill us?" she hiccupped in a thick Irish accent.

Rip said nothing as he slid out of the saddle. He stood over the woman, drunk on power, as he watched her cry. His gloved hand stroked her cheek, and she flinched away from his touch.

"Unfortunately for you, miss, you've seen my face," Rip replied with a twisted grin on his handsome face. He looked to her right and saw her husband—who had all but wet his trousers at the sight of Rip's revolver. He pulled back on the hammer and shot the man dead.

The woman's scream broke through the trees and echoed off the cliffs. She screamed with all her might until Rip smashed the butt end of his gun against her head.

"Shut up," he snarled. Blood oozed from a cut on her forehead. Rip held his gun to her temple and said, "I'm going to make this very simple. Either you can fight this and end up like your husband. Or you can tell us where the money is, and I might let you live."

"Under the seat!"

That, of course, had been a lie. Rip had no intention of keeping the woman alive, but he enjoyed the hope that blossomed in her eyes—hope he extinguished with a single bullet. He sighed as the woman's body fell into her husband.

Sal and the others looked at him in shock. Rip ignored their open-mouthed stares and climbed into the back of the stagecoach.

There was a notch in the wood where his hand brushed. He pushed his finger in the hole and pulled up the seat. They lifted the wood off the bench, and beneath it was a hidden strongbox. It seemed Pratt & Dempcy hadn't gotten rid of all of Budd Mansfield's ideas. Rip shot the lock on the box and kicked it open.

Inside were several stacks of cash, the deed to some land, bearer bonds, and a small sack of jewels. It was a good payday. He pocketed the jewels and the deed before he stepped out of the stagecoach. "Get rid of these bodies in the river," Rip said. "And empty that box." He stepped over the husband and felt a hand grab his ankle.

The woman was alive.

Rip said nothing to his men. He shook off her hold and walked back to Storm. The large stallion lipped at his hand. Rip listened to the sound of the bodies hitting the water.

Part of him hoped the woman survived. The other half of him delighted in nothing more than the thought of her dying, with his smiling face being the last thing she saw.

"This ain't like you, Rip," said Charles suddenly. "Since when do you kill in cold blood? I'd expect somethin' like this from Sal, but not from you."

"Time changes us all, but I only kill out of necessity," he explained. "She saw my face. I would not let her live, let her jeopardize everything I've worked for."

Rip could tell his reasoning hadn't quite convinced Charles. Still, he lifted himself onto Storm's back, and they rode back to the Old Mill with the loot in hand.

Chapter 9

"We need to hurry," Blake said as he watched the front door. "They'll be back any minute once they've figured out it was a distraction."

"I'm going as quickly as I can." Budd turned the dial on the safe. He pressed his ear to the metal, listening for ticks as he tried to crack the combination. "Now shut up so I can concentrate. Or do you want to give it a go?"

Blake lifted his hands in surrender.

A third explosion came from the mountains. Budd stiffened. There hadn't been a third explosion in the plan. He took it for what it was... a warning.

Budd worked hard at cracking the safe, doubling his efforts until he heard the lock click. He threw open the door and found the ledger. Inside was a detailed list of all the stolen loot, transport dates, and plans for the robberies.

The log included information on each of Pratt & Dempcy's stagecoaches that had been attacked, as well as a plot to kill the mayor and take over Sacramento.

Budd shoved the ledger into his satchel. He prayed to God that Evan had made it off the mountain as he ran out of the loot room. Blake and Steven followed. They entered the main space just as the large door opened.

Budd ducked behind an old interior wall and cocked his rifle. Six outlaws entered the building with their guns drawn. There was no way out.

His eyes peered through the shadows, taking in his surroundings. He knew they would have to fight their way out. The bandits huddled together and moved as a group.

Budd had to separate them. He carefully stepped out from behind his cover and fired his gun.

The bandits scattered like the vermin they were. Blake took down the first one. He threw his body at the bandit and knocked him to the ground. They wrestled over the bandit's gun, rolling on the floor of the Old Mill.

Steven jumped onto the back of the second man while Budd sent the others running for cover with some well-aimed shots from his rifle. Three of the bandits escaped out into the courtyard.

Budd tracked another with his eyes. He lunged at the bandit and bashed him in the face with his rifle.

"You don't know who you're stealin' from," gargled the bandit. His nose was leaning at an awkward angle as blood poured down his face. "Ripley Eagleson, don't take too kindly to folks takin' what belongs to him."

Budd ducked before the bandit could punch him. He sidestepped a second attack and shot the bandit in the leg with his rifle. The bandit crumpled to the floor in pain, gripping his injured leg with pale fingers.

Budd left the man on the ground, where he landed and exited the building. He stepped out into the courtyard and came under fire.

Bullets hit the wooden door and lodged themselves in the timbers behind Budd. He scrambled on his hands and knees for cover.

There was a worker's cart near the entrance of the Old Mill. It would have to do. He vaulted over a barrel and raced across the courtyard.

His boot sank into an uneven part of the terrain, and he fell. Budd rolled behind the cart and looked down at his twisted ankle. He cursed his foul luck under his breath and reloaded his rifle.

Blake and Steven joined the fight in the courtyard a moment later. The brothers returned fire while Budd got his bearings. He surveyed the area and spotted the three remaining bandits crouched behind a wagon that had been stripped back to the framing.

He leaned over the cart and took aim, staring down the sights as sweat dripped down his temple. Budd pulled back on the hammer and shot with deadly aim. A bandit spun with the force of the bullet and dropped.

The other two retreated to the stables.

Budd heard horses approaching and whistled for Blake and Steven. "Get down!" he shouted only seconds before the gate came crashing down. A swarm of outlaws flooded into the courtyard.

Budd changed cover, dashing toward the stables as a hailstorm of bullets rained down upon him. One shot hit its mark. Budd felt heat explode across his arm, and he hit the wall of the stables hard. The air was punched from his lungs upon impact.

Steven grabbed Budd and pulled him inside before Blake shut the stable doors. Budd pulled his pistol from its holster and shot down the two bandits that hid in a nearby stall. He collapsed against Steven and caught his breath. His hands trembled as waves of pain crashed over him. "Any sign of Evan?" Budd asked. "He should be down the mountain by now."

"No. He ain't here as far as I saw, but it was hard to see in all the smoke." Steven propped Budd up against the stall and used a bandana to tie off his arm. The bullet had hit Budd in the shoulder, just inches from his heart. It had been close to a grim end for Budd Mansfield, but God seemed to be on their side that day.

Luck, however, was not.

"How many are there?" Budd asked through gritted teeth. "Looked like a dang army."

"Could be twelve. Could be fifteen," Blake replied with a shrug. "Either we find a way out of here, or we lay down our guns now."

"We have come too far to die now," Budd said. "And we ain't giving up, either. We keep fighting until help comes for us."

Steven shook his head. "Could be days before anyone investigates the explosions or Evan can get help. We'll run out of bullets before then. Besides, what's stopping them from bustin' in here right now?"

"Ripley Eagleson."

The brothers looked at Budd as though he had gone mad.

"They know we took something of his," Budd explained. "They know I'm here and that Rip will want to punish me for it himself. They can't kill me. Not without angering Rip."

***

Yosemite Valley, California

Rip and Salazar rode ahead. They reached the outskirts of Yosemite Valley with time left to spare. There was less than a day's ride back to the Old Mill.

"Do you have a problem with what happened back there?" Rip asked Sal. "With the killing, I mean. I know you don't like to kill women…"

"You do not care what I think," Sal replied. "You give me orders and expect obedience. Leave it the way it is."

"But—"

There was a fierce rumble through the forest.

Smoke appeared on the horizon. Ripley Eagleson pulled his horse to a stop and watched as birds scattered across the sky. Large clouds of smoke came from the western mountains where the bandit camp was situated.

A curse dripped from his lips. "Back to the Old Mill!" Rip shouted to his men. "Go now!" He bucked in the saddle and urged Storm on. The large stallion kicked into a run, roaring down the path within minutes.

Gunshots were heard over the sound of panicked shouts.

A stampede of footfalls came from the bandit camp as men rushed to put out the flames caused by the explosions. Rip climbed down from his horse and pushed his way into the center of the camp, where most of the bandits had gathered. Isiah West grabbed the man nearest to him and demanded answers.

Rip overheard talk of Budd Mansfield having been trapped in the Old Mill, and Rip's stomach sank. Had he gone for the ledger? Surely there is no way Mansfield could have known about the ledger, Rip thought. But what other reason would the man have for being at the Old Mill?

Rip searched the camp for weapons. He found an old Winchester rifle and a few pistols, handing them to his men before he led them to the Old Mill. It was a shock to his system when he saw someone had torn the gate down and there was an all-out war in the courtyard. "Stop!" he ordered. "Stop!"

"It's Mansfield," someone said. "He's in the stables."

"I said stop!"

Gunshots trickled off into silence. Rip's ears rang from the cacophony of noise he had walked into. He gestured for the gang to follow. Salazar and Charles flanked his advances. They stayed close to Rip as he approached the stables, arms raised and his gun holstered.

"You come out of there, Budd Mansfield," Rip said calmly. "There's no reason for you to die today."

The window above the stable doors opened. Mansfield's rifle appeared. Sunlight glinted off the barrel as the man fearlessly took aim right at Rip. "Oh, I don't think I will."

"You've been holed up in there for what? A day now? Maybe two? Let's talk this out." Rip stepped over bodies as he neared the stables. Budd Mansfield and his men were skilled killers, despite their twisted sense of justice.

Each step he took was a gruesome reminder that he had a gun aimed at his chest. He stopped when he heard the rifle cock. "Either you'll tire out or run out of ammunition. But we can stop that from happening. Just give me back whatever you took, and I'll let you walk out of here… alive."

Rip's answer came when Budd Mansfield fired at the ground by his feet.

He jumped back and snarled, "Fine! Have it your way." Rip lifted his arm to give the signal for his men to shoot, but he heard a quiet sizzle nearby.

He looked back toward the gate and saw Evan Farris with a stick of dynamite in his hand. The insufferable man tossed the stick through the air and it landed near Isiah West's bandits. A flash of light and a cloud of gunpowder obscured Rip's vision. He flew across the courtyard and landed near the mill.

The ringing in his ears worsened.

Budd Mansfield picked off the bandits one by one with his rifle. Evan Farris ran into the cloud of smoke and gunpowder without fear and tackled Salazar Torez to the ground.

Steven and Blake Wright fired their pistols from the stable doors. The explosion drew unwanted attention. Through the chaos, Rip spotted the two Pinkertons as they joined the fight.

The two men must have been patrolling the roads when they heard the explosions, just as Rip had.

He quickly realized he was soon to be outnumbered by Budd Mansfield and his men. Rip attempted to stand, only to realize he had been impaled on a bit of shrapnel. He clenched his teeth and yanked himself free.

A scream bubbled up from the depths of his soul, but Rip bit down on his tongue to keep it at bay. His legs nearly gave out beneath him as he stumbled to his feet. He pressed his hand to his wound and entered the Old Mill.

Hidden in the loot room was a secret door behind the safe. Rip used all of his strength to push the safe aside. Nausea burned at the back of his throat. Stars danced in his vision.

He sucked in a sharp breath and pulled open the secret hatch that led to the ravine. On his hands and knees, he crawled until he heard water rushing all around him.

Daylight breached the wall. Rip kicked his way through a grate and found himself near the abandoned bandit camp. To his surprise, Storm still waited near the edge of the camp.

Rip whistled for his steed. The large horse trotted over. He gripped the saddle horn, placed his foot in the stirrup, and hoisted himself into the saddle. Rip panted heavily.

His chest heaved, and dark spots appeared in his vision. Storm shuffled in place, jostling Rip in a way that caused a fresh wave of nausea that coursed through him. Once his head stopped spinning, he eased Storm away from the Old Mill and headed west toward Timber.

Chapter 10

"So you thought you could come here and take what is ours," Sal said as he stood over a battered Evan Farris, who looked only seconds away from death. "But I will kill you and your partner before I allow that to happen. I need that money."

"That's blood money in there, and you know it." Evan spat blood onto the ground and wheezed as he stood up. There was a pale cast on the man's face, but he never once gave up. Instead, he picked up a fiery plank of wood left in the explosion's aftermath and wielded it like a weapon. "Besides, we ain't here for the loot."

"Coming here was foolish no matter the reason," Sal huffed. "Because I remember you. I was there the day that John Pepper killed tu familia. And I laughed as they called out for you."

"My… my wife… she…"

"You could have saved them, you know," he taunted. "But you were too weak."

Evan swung the wood as Sal slashed toward him with his knife. Sal grabbed the burning plank with his bare hand and cut Evan across the face. The two of them stumbled back.

Salazar felt as though he were on fire as he looked down at his burned hand and cursed. The skin was red and covered with angry blisters. He fell to the ground and searched for his boss.

Ripley Eagleson was nowhere in sight. Sal half hoped his boss had perished in the explosion, but just as the smoke cleared, he glimpsed Rip as he fled. "Coward," Sal snarled as he attempted to stand.

Evan Farris had been right behind him, ready to knock him back down. He stared up into glacier blue eyes and wrapped his hand around his knife. Sal slashed viciously at Evan's legs. Budd Mansfield's partner leaped out of the way of the blade.

Sal used the distance between them and stood up to his full height. He charged toward Evan like a bull and they crashed into the stables. The smell of horse dung stung his nose, something fierce, mingling with the scent of gunpowder and blood. Charred splinters of wood surrounded them.

Sal buried his knife into Evan's thigh, causing the man to shriek in pain as Isiah and Charles entered the stables behind them. Steven Wright and Isiah West collided in a fit of violence that sent both men careening toward the ground.

Charles and Blake Wright circled one another like vultures as Budd Mansfield limped out into the courtyard. Mansfield was most likely aware that Rip had fled rather than die like a man.

A flash of pain brought Sal's attention back to the fight. He dodged the next blow and landed one of his own. Though the pain in his burned hand took the heft out of his punches, Sal's attack never stopped.

He battered his fists into Evan Farris's face until the man pulled the knife from his leg and pressed it against Sal's throat. Sal stilled. He lifted his arms in surrender, but there was something dark in Evan Farris's gaze that he recognized. It was the same look that came over Sal whenever he took a life.

And it was then he knew one of them wouldn't walk away from the fight. "You want to kill me, gringo?" Sal chuckled harshly. "Then do it."

"Why? Why did John's gang attack our settlement?"

His legs trembled as he pulled to his feet. "We had nothing better to do."

"You watched as he killed my wife and child," Evan said in disbelief. "And you did nothing to stop him... because it was fun?"

Evan Farris towered over him like a warrior, and Sal respected him for not cowering like so many had before. But Sal was not afraid of the large man. He unsheathed his second knife and tossed it into the air.

Evan looked up at the twirling blade. Sal used the distraction and rammed his knee into Evan's stomach. The knife hit the dirt near the stable wall. Evan doubled over. He dropped to his knees in front of Sal as he coughed raggedly.

"Things could have been different if you had not joined up with Budd Mansfield," Salazar said. "You could have joined us and lived your life as the man you were meant to be."

"I would rather die than join you..."

"Do not say such things," he chuckled. "Or they might come true."

"I'm not afraid of death," Evan retorted. "And I ain't afraid of you, either."

"You should be."

"Why? Why should I fear a man who was so easily conned by Ripley Eagleson?" Evan pressed a hand to his side and grimaced. "He played you like a fiddle."

"What are you talking about?"

"The money," Evan replied. "Your families haven't seen a dime. Ripley Eagleson has it all stashed away in Reno. He never intended to protect your family, Salazar. And thanks to his sister agreeing to work with us, the money'll soon be returned to its rightful owners."

Sal picked up his discarded blade and walked toward Evan Farris once more. But the force of a bullet in his chest stopped him short. He looked down as a dark stain spread across his torso and his knees buckled.

Sal hadn't noticed when Evan had grabbed his gun from the holster. He fell face down in the dirt, took one deep breath, and exhaled for the last time. Darkness flooded his sight and the last thought that crossed his mind was not of his family but of the betrayal he felt at the knowledge of what Rip had done.

***

Budd heard a gunshot nearby.

He pushed himself into an upright position. Bullets dropped to the floor as he attempted to reload his rifle. He bit down on his lip to keep from screaming, but the pain in his shoulder was too much. A pained groan tumbled from his mouth.

He dropped the heavy rifle, and it clattered to the floor where he had been perched in the loft of the stables. Budd crawled through the tight space and lowered himself down the ladder, one rung at a time. His boots hit the ground, but his body betrayed him, and he collapsed against the ladder.

Sweat trickled down his forehead and soaked into the collar of his shirt. Budd took peace in the silence outside, for he knew it marked an end to the fighting.

Whether or not they were safe remained to be seen. He shuffled away from the ladder and walked over to where Evan leaned against the stable wall. "You all right?" he asked as his gaze landed on Evan.

Salazar Torez's body lay unmoving near Evan's feet. There were tears in Budd's partner's eyes. "I will be," Evan said. "You all right?"

"I've survived worse. It ain't as bad as the last time I was shot in this arm." Budd wiped his brow and limped over to his friend. He offered Evan a hand, but it was swatted away as Budd was in no condition to be of help to anybody. "Any sign of Blake or Steven?"

"They were out in the courtyard last I saw."

Budd nodded and walked over to the doors of the stables. He used his good shoulder and nudged them open wider. The fight had come to a gruesome end.

Bodies littered the ground, and the stench of blood was everywhere. Jack Graham and Lucas Smith stood near the gate, with their guns drawn and matching frowns on their faces. Dawson entered the courtyard with Mayor Thomas and Marshal Greene.

Out of dozens of bandits, only seven remained. They laid down their weapons when they noticed Budd had survived and Ripley Eagleson was no longer in sight.

"I got help when I heard the explosions," Dawson said as he walked over to Budd. "I'm sorry I wasn't here when you needed me. I just…"

"You're here now," Budd replied. "That's all that matters." He stepped around Dawson and approached Marshal Greene.

The ledger was retrieved from his satchel and handed over to the lawman.

Greene scowled down at the ledger and opened the cover. "What is this?"

"Everything you need to prove Ripley Eagleson was behind the stagecoach robberies, the killings, and the attack on Sacramento and Black Lake," Budd answered. "And Beatrice Pepper, Ripley Eagleson's sister, will testify it's all true."

There was suddenly a stunned expression on Marshal Greene's face. "Coming here was the bravest or the stupidest thing you ever did. What would you have done if we hadn't been in the valley and caught up with Dawson?"

"I would have fought until my last breath," Budd said honestly, for he had been willing to die in order to get justice. "The question now is, what do you intend to do now that you have this ledger? I'm an innocent man, Marshal, and I hope to live out the rest of my days as such."

Marshal Greene read the name branded on the inside of the leather cover. He flipped through the pages haphazardly, scanning the information with almost disinterest gleaming in his eyes. But there was no denying the truth hidden in those pages—a truth that a lawman like Marshal Greene couldn't ignore.

"Do you got a witness?" asked the marshal. "Because most of the victims in the robberies have either been killed or they've identified you."

"We have two witnesses," Budd answered. "Beatrice Pepper and Pete Jones." He saw the names further shocked the marshal. But there was something other than surprise behind the man's expression. Perhaps it was... respect?

Mayor Thomas took the ledger from the lawman's hand and took great care in reading some pages. He stepped forward and laid a hand on Budd's good arm. "I want to say that I'm sorry I doubted you. I shouldn't have believed that... that monster. They should hang him for what he's done, and I sincerely apologize."

"Just make sure Ripley Eagleson pays for what he has done." Budd shrugged off the mayor's hand and limped past both men.

He met with Blake and Steven beyond the gate, where they shared a cigarette between them. It wasn't long before Evan joined them. They then sat in silent companionship as the world moved on around them.

Budd pressed a hand to his wound and hissed. He needed a doctor, and fast. "Where are the horses?"

"Up the path a few paces," Evan replied. "They got spooked when the explosions started."

He led them to the mounts as Budd leaned on Steven for support. Blake and Steven helped Budd and Evan into their saddles before they climbed onto their own horses.

"What happened to Charles?" Budd asked Blake.

"He slipped away when Evan blew the courtyard to pieces," Blake answered with a pointed glare at Evan. "But I'm glad he did. The fight wasn't goin' in my favor. Charles fights dirty, and he's built like an ox."

"Eagleson escaped as well." Budd's admission brought him great shame. He should have caught Ripley Eagleson. "We'll head to Sacramento and settle things with Marshal Greene. And then we're going after Eagleson and Charles."

"Seeing Dawson was a surprise," Steven said. "I expected him to be halfway to Reno by now. His conscience finally got to him, I guess.

"I don't know," Budd sighed. "Dawson had his reasons for wanting to leave. I just hope he remembers who helped to clear his good name. You boys deserve a reward, at the very least. Me? I want little. I just need to breathe air as a free man again."

Chapter 11

Timber, California

Rain trickled from the sky as the temperature dropped. The sun disappeared behind a spattering of dark clouds that moved toward the mountains. Ripley Eagleson dug through his saddlebag for an old shirt and tied it around his waist to stop the bleeding.

He prayed to God that he made it out of the valley alive. His wound throbbed beneath the waterlogged fabric of his shirt. Rain sloshed over his shoulders and matted his hair to the side of his face. He shivered from the frigid air that whipped through the trees. Thunder rumbled from up high.

Storm crossed the ravine slowly, trudging through the cold shallows. The mount walked along the rocky riverbed until they reached the other side. Rip held on tight as they traveled over hills, through valleys, and across large expansions of tall grass.

He gripped the reins with white knuckles and glanced over his shoulder from time to time, ensuring no one had followed him. Nearly two days passed before they reached town.

Rip turned Storm toward the general store. He tumbled from the saddle gracelessly and hobbled over to the door. No one was working at the late hour that Rip rode into

Timber, so he smashed the window on the door with his elbow.

A quick flick of the lock and he was inside. He grabbed a bottle of whiskey, a sewing needle, thread, and bandages. Hell, he was half tempted just to use a hot poker and seal the wound shut, but he didn't think he could stand the pain.

The walk over to the saloon was agonizing for Rip. He pushed his way through the swinging doors and the music stopped. "Give me my old room," he barked at the owner.

The older man gestured to Bill behind the bar before he tossed the key to Rip. He caught the key in one hand and carried his supplies up the stairs. Folks stared openly as he slinked down the hallway.

The door to the bedchamber opened with a bang, smacking against the wall. Rip hurried and closed the door behind him before he dumped his supplies on the bed. He pulled back his coat and tore open his shirt. The wound looked vile. His trembling fingers prodded along the edges that had grown oddly numb during his ride into town.

He unbuckled his belt and shoved it between his teeth. Rip splashed liquor onto the wound and cleared away the debris that had gotten inside. He bit down on the belt and screamed through tightly clenched teeth. Lightheaded and weak, Rip sewed his wound shut.

Luckily, the shrapnel that had impaled him hadn't gone all the way through. He fell back onto the bed and allowed the belt to slip free. The pain subsided as he drifted off.

But sleep didn't last for more than an hour, for Rip awakened by the sound of his window opening. He reached for his revolver, but a hand clamped tightly onto his wrist. Charles.

Rip breathed a sigh of relief. "How many survived?" Rip asked.

"Just me," Charles replied grimly. "Salazar and the others didn't make it. I got out of there when those darn Pinkertons arrived. Where were you?"

Rip gestured to his battered body. "I got hit bad in the explosion. Had to get out of there."

Charles nodded, seeming to understand why Rip had abandoned them when he had. "Mansfield and my brothers are still alive. That partner of his, too. What are we goin' to do about it? We can't just let 'em put the law on us again."

Rip shook his head. He was out of brilliant plans. His focus was merely on survival. Budd Mansfield was sure to come after him once his wounds healed. Rip needed to get out of Timber as fast as he could.

"We have to lie low," he said finally. "Gather our strength and regroup. We have allies out in Nevada."

Charles glared at Rip with a hatred that was so uncharacteristic it took Rip by surprise. "So... your big plan is to run? Hide like some sort of coward? I ain't no—"

"Now, you hold on one second," Rip snapped, cutting off Charles's outburst. "I ain't no coward, and I never will be. All I'm saying is we need to do this the right way and stay out of trouble until things calm down."

That seemed to quell some of the hatred in Charles, at least for the time being. The outlaw was unpredictable at the best of times and downright mad at his worst. Charles sat on the edge of the bed and took a long look at Rip's side, where the shrapnel had pierced him.

He hissed sympathetically. "That don't look good, boss."

"I'll live," Rip grumbled. "But I need you to do something for me. It'll be dangerous, but we'll need it if we intend to survive until we reach Nevada."

"What is it?"

Rip pointed to his bag on the floor beside the entrance.

Charles got up and moseyed over. He picked the bag up and handed it to Rip. Inside was a map of Sacramento. It had circled one area in particular. The mayor's house. It seemed impossible to even imagine breaking into the mayor's house, but it was Rip's last hope.

"There's a small box of golden nuggets stashed in the mayor's study. It's hidden in a safe behind the shelf of books," Rip told Charles. "We break in, take the box, and leave for Nevada before anyone is the wiser."

Charles looked uneasy. The outlaw fidgeted with the cuff of his jacket, flicking the button over and over until it looked as though it might pop off. "All right," he answered hesitantly. "We can do it when the mayor holds the election for sheriff at city hall."

***

Sacramento, California

Budd's shallow breaths caused the linens to slip down his torso, exposing the bare, scarred skin and bandages. A soft voice spoke, but his groggy mind failed to make out the words. He opened his eyes and his heart skipped a beat.

Dorothy Valentine sat on the edge of his cot with a look of concern on her lovely face. Budd stared openly, for he hadn't realized just how much he missed her. He pulled the covers higher, but she stopped him.

Her small hand touched the bandage on his shoulder. "How many times are you goin' to risk your life to find Ripley Eagleson?" she asked quietly. "When I heard you had been shot… Just don't let this consume you any more than it already has."

"I'm not after vengeance or anything. I want justice for all the people he's wronged."

"The Pinkertons can handle it," she argued. "Let them retrieve the stolen loot and find Ripley Eagleson."

Budd shook his head and ran his fingers through his hair. "I can't. Jack says he has his hands full already with the investigation, and Marshal Greene is still looking into what happened at the Old Mill."

"Then let Ike Smith handle it," she suggested. Ike Smith was a good man, a former U.S. Marshal, and a candidate for sheriff. "He'll do it the right way and… and I don't lay awake at night, hopin' he ain't gotten himself killed."

Budd sat up on the cot and grabbed his shirt from the back of the chair beside the bed. "I need to have a talk with the sheriff." He awkwardly pushed the shirt up over his arms and situated it over the bandages.

Dotty helped him do up the buttons as he stood up and then tucked the shirt into his trousers. Once he was dressed, they walked out of the physician's office and onto the streets. Dotty tucked her hand into the crook of his elbow and leaned her head on his good shoulder.

They made their way down to the sheriff's office where Dawson and the other two candidates for sheriff waited. Budd greeted the men with a round of handshakes.

He knew Dawson and Ike Smith, but there was something about Nigel Hermon that rubbed Budd the wrong way. He was familiar, even though Budd couldn't quite place him.

"Have a seat, Mr. Mansfield," Nigel Hermon, the temporary sheriff, said. "We need to go over a few things before the marshal arrives."

Budd took Dotty's hand and sat in the offered chair stiffly. He squeezed her hand for comfort, and she returned the gesture reassuringly. His eyes met Dawson's across the room.

The man looked uncomfortable, to say the least. Budd could tell something was wrong in the way Dawson's shoulders had slumped forward, the tension around his mouth, and the deadened look in his gaze.

"What is it you want from me?" Budd asked. "Haven't I already proved my innocence?"

"Yes, you have," Nigel Hermon replied. "But this is about you unnecessarily putting your life in danger by hunting him down yourself. You're not a bounty hunter, and you ain't a lawman, Mr. Mansfield. I cannot—and will not—allow a citizen of this town to undermine my—"

"Do you agree with this?" Budd asked Dawson, cutting off the temporary sheriff.

"They outvoted me," Dawson answered. "There's no moving them on this, Budd. Until the election is over, I have little say in the matter."

Ike Smith lifted his hands as if Budd were a wild animal in need of calming. "They might acquit you of the charges against you, but the townsfolk don't know whether they can trust you. They would much rather have this matter attended to by the law."

"Lately, I ain't putting much faith in the law." Budd stood up to leave, but he stopped beside the door. He looked down at Dotty's hand clasped in his own and sighed heavily. "Ripley Eagleson is afraid of me. He'll mess up, and I plan on being there when it happens."

"He's long gone by now," Nigel Hermon claimed. "We missed our shot at catching him when you allowed him to escape the Old Mill."

Budd dropped Dotty's hand and stormed over to Nigel. He grabbed the foolish man by the front of his coat and lifted him off his feet. Budd slammed Nigel against the wall with so much force that the plaster cracked.

"When I allowed him to escape? I was bleeding out in a stable when Ripley Eagleson ran like a coward! We were fighting for our lives like we always have. Where was the law then, huh?"

Dawson and Ike Smith pulled Budd off Nigel. Pain shot up his arm, and he nearly fell over. Bile burned his throat as he fought back a scream. The lawmen released him quickly, most likely having seen his pained expression. Budd huffed loudly as he tried to regain his control.

Dotty was by his side in an instant. She pressed her forehead to his. "Easy, Budd," she whispered between them. "Nice and slow."

He breathed slowly, filling his senses with all that was Dorothy Valentine.

At least until Ike Smith tugged him aside. He opened the drawer of the sheriff's desk and pulled something free. It was a deputy badge. "If you really intend to help, then we need to do this the right way."

Chapter 12

Three days had come and gone without a word from Charles. Rip sipped his coffee and quietly contemplated what might have delayed the outlaw. He finished writing his letters to his allies and then left his room.

The ladies in the corridor cooed as he walked by. Rip flashed them a charming grin and tipped his hat. He moseyed down to the bar where the saloon owner and Bill served drinks to numerous patrons.

The smell of liquor and sweat filled the air. Rip grimaced as he paid the saloon owner for another week's stay in his usual room. The man didn't seem pleased, but he was far too frightened to deny Rip. In fact, most people had lost their respect for him, but the fear they felt remained strong.

"Good evenin', Mr. Eagleson," Bill murmured from behind the bar. "Any plans for the night? Or are you just comin' down here for a drink?"

"I have a meeting with an associate of mine."

"It's a bit late for business, don't you think?"

Rip shook his head. "This can't wait," he replied simply. "Besides, there are things I need to get before I leave town for a while."

Bill reached beneath the counter and then placed a wanted poster on the bar. "Does this have anythin' to do with why you are leavin'?"

His own face stared up at him from the poster. He was wanted for murder, robbery, and a slew of other unsavory crimes. Rip saw the price on his head was enough to make anybody feel tempted.

He glanced over his shoulder and noticed just how many of the saloon goers had their eyes on him. All of them had a lust for money in their eyes.

Suddenly, the jovial atmosphere didn't feel so friendly. Rip slid the poster across the bar along with a few dollars for Bill to keep quiet. He then walked out the back door and into the alleyway where he had been instructed to meet his man.

The lamp above his head flickered each time the wind blew. Loud voices from the saloon carried through the alleyway, echoing off the buildings. Somewhere in the distance, a dog barked continuously.

Ripley Eagleson waited for nearly four hours before his contact showed up. He stamped out his cigar on the railing beside his arm and gestured for his companion to come closer. Nigel Hermon stepped into the light and frowned at Rip.

"What's the matter?" Rip asked incredulously. "Don't tell me you forgot to stall the election."

"No, no. It'll happen next week as we planned," Nigel replied. "But we got a problem."

"What sort of problem?"

"It's Budd Mansfield."

Rip pinched the bridge of his nose and breathed deeply, trying in vain to calm his frustration. "He's supposed to be dead," Rip said. "Your letter said he was near death."

"I thought the infection would do the job, but he's stronger than I suspected," Hermon replied. He wiped his sleeve across his brow and leaned in closer to Rip. "He's been talking about hunting you down. The others support him. I don't know how much longer—"

Rip held his hand up and cut off the would-be sheriff's words. "You work for me, understand? You will hold off this election for as long as I see fit. And when you are sheriff, you will clear my good name."

"But the mayor no longer supports you, Rip," Nigel said. "He's hosting a dinner in Budd Mansfield's honor tomorrow night. It's supposed to be the event of the year."

Rip whirled around and kicked the wall behind him. He gripped his injured side and cursed. "They can't just throw me away," he growled. "My money and excellent reputation helped make the city what it is! They owe me!"

Nigel shook his head and shrugged. "They don't need you anymore. They have deputized Budd Mansfield to sanction your arrest."

Anger took over Rip, claiming his mind with a darkness that ran deep in his soul. He pulled out his revolver and shot Nigel dead. Three bullets. That was all it had taken to claim the man's life. The body dropped to the ground, blocking the exit to the alley.

Rip tucked an ace of spades in Nigel Hermon's pocket and stepped over him with a blank expression on his face. He walked along the winding alley until he reached a door hidden in the shadows of a staircase. Rip knocked three times in rapid succession.

The door opened. Dale and Merl Murphy allowed Rip to enter without question, for their cousin Leroy had once been a loyal member of the Blood Eagles. Though Dale was the preacher's son, he was just as crooked as the rest of the Murphy family. So much so that Rip knew he could count on Dale for the job ahead.

He hovered inside the entrance of their small home behind the gun shop and placed a stack of money on the table near the door.

Merl whistled in appreciation. "That's a lot of cash, Rip."

"And there's more where that came from if you succeed," he told them. "The mayor and the rest of Sacramento have to be distracted. Do whatever it takes, but do it and get out of town quickly, before anyone is the wiser."

"What about that Budd Mansfield? Ain't he lookin' for you?" Merl asked with a scoff. He then looked at the money on the table. "Seems to me like you need us more than we need you."

"Budd Mansfield is not a problem. If you see him, shoot him." Rip picked up the cash he had set down, added a few more dollars, and then handed it to Merl.

Dale had already begun to polish his gun. The Murphy boys seemed eager to start, which was what Rip had been counting on. He told them the details of the plan and paid them extra to move the body out of the alleyway.

***

Sacramento, California

The city was quiet in the early hours of the morning. Dew clung to the blades of grass near the front door. Frost covered the shutters on the windows. A cool breeze rustled the tree that cast a shadow upon a little blue house.

Budd Mansfield and Evan Farris stepped outside of their front door just as the sun rose. The night had been filled with bad dreams, tossing and turning without end. Dark circles rested beneath Budd's eyes. He yawned loudly, stretching his mouth open wide before he let out a groan that came from somewhere down deep inside.

Folks still avoided him as he passed by on the street. He kept his head held high and his shoulders squared. Budd walked with the confident swagger they had once known him for.

His striking gaze flickered over every face in the crowd, for he half expected Ripley Eagleson to appear out of nowhere. Was it paranoia or something in his gut that tried to warn him? Budd wasn't sure, but he couldn't shake the feeling that the fight wasn't over—that Ripley Eagleson might have had one more ace up his sleeve.

Still, there was a slight smile on Budd's face as he made his way down to the sheriff's office.

"What are you so happy about?" Evan asked. "You barely survived that bout of infection a few days ago."

"For the first time in a long time, I feel like we might just win this," Budd answered honestly. "The odds are in our favor, and we got Eagleson on the run. Before now, there wasn't really much reason to smile. But today marks the turning of the tides."

Evan chuckled and clapped Budd on the back. They pushed their way inside the sheriff's office. Dotty served coffee with small clumps of sugar as Dawson and Ike talked quietly with the Pinkertons. There was a pinched expression on Jack Graham's face that stole Budd's smile away.

Budd took a seat next to Beatrice Pepper and awaited what he assumed was bad news. Sure enough, the Pinkerton detective reached into his pocket and brought out a blood-stained ace of spades that was all too familiar to Budd.

"Nigel Hermon is dead. They found him last night in Timber with three bullets in his chest," Graham told Budd. "Mayor Thomas wants to postpone the election for sheriff until after the funeral, so the family has time to mourn his loss."

"Sacramento can't be lawless for that long," Budd replied. "What does the marshal have to say about any of this? Can't he look after the city until we get a sheriff?"

"He plans to do whatever he can to make this a smooth transition, but there isn't much he can do with Ripley Eagleson out there. The marshal is using all his resources trying to find where Eagleson has been hiding, and no one outside of this room will talk."

"I don't care what he's doing. He can't just leave Sacramento at a time like this. It's leaving the city open to another attack." Budd tossed his hat on the ground and tugged at his hair. He looked up at the Pinkertons and the two men, hoping to get elected as sheriff.

The badge pinned to his coat felt heavy suddenly. Was that what it meant to be a lawman? To be held back by unseen laws and obligations that kept a man from doing everything in his power to set things right? Budd wasn't so sure he wanted the badge, not if it meant his hands were tied.

"Ripley Eagleson is getting what he wants. You know that, right? He wants this city unprotected. He wants chaos."

Marshal Greene entered the sheriff's office. The room went quiet. Though Budd had his own opinions where the marshal was concerned, he couldn't deny just how rundown the lawman appeared to be.

Hell, he looked about as exhausted as Budd felt. It seemed Budd wasn't the only person losing sleep over Ripley Eagleson and what the outlaw might do next.

"I will handle Ripley Eagleson, Mansfield," said Marshal Greene. "Meanwhile, you are expected to appear at the mayor's dinner social tomorrow night. It is important we show a united front to the people, despite how divided we might be on the subject of Ripley Eagleson. I, for one, do not want a citywide panic getting in my way."

"They deputized me for a reason."

"And when I require your help, I will send word. Until then, you patrol the city with everyone else." Marshal Greene walked past Budd and greeted Beatrice and Dotty with a smile that would have made a politician proud.

But Budd saw the hollowness behind the marshal's eyes. It told him the marshal already considered Ripley Eagleson gone for good.

Budd kicked to his feet and stormed out. He stomped across the dirt road and shoved his way into the saloon. "One hundred dollars to any man willing to tell me what happened to Nigel Hermon," Budd said as he slammed the money on the bar. A man to his left perked up at the sight of the money and waved Budd over. "You get the money after I get my information."

"Rip shot him," slurred the man. "Killed him out back."

"You saw it?"

The drunken man nodded his head. "Heard him talkin' about meetin' a-an associate of his, so I followed him. Sheriff Hermon and Rip started arguin' about the election."

"Did they say why the election was important?" Budd asked.

"No," the man said. "Just that it needed to be stalled until next week."

"Thank you, sir. I appreciate you taking this risk." Budd slid the hundred dollars over and left the saloon.

Evan stood outside with a knowing expression on his face. He must have suspected Budd wouldn't have been able to sit by and wait as Ripley Eagleson plotted the city's demise. "I take it you got what you came for? Where to now, Budd?"

"The tailor," Budd grumbled irritably. "I need a suit."

Chapter 13

Sacramento, California

Voices murmured when Budd stepped through the front door. He was dressed in his best suit with his arm in a sling.

Heads turned in his direction as he approached the mayor. Mayor Thomas shook Budd's hand and bowed his head to Dotty—who looked stunning in her blue dress with yellow lace. She beamed at Budd's side, positively glowing with happiness. Budd envied her.

Half the city showed up to the mayor's dinner social hoping to get a look at Budd. He was still the talk of the town, despite being declared innocent of Ripley Eagleson's crimes. In fact, it was as if he were some sort of circus animal being paraded around for everyone to gawk at.

He was thankful Dotty had agreed to accompany him to the dinner. She was his rock through all the chaos that had followed the battle at the Old Mill.

He was beyond grateful for her presence, though he wished he had been stronger where Dotty was concerned. Love—or something like it—had swept him away like a fierce storm, and he was helpless to do anything about it.

The thought of being helpless for any reason often angered Budd. However, the thought of being at the mercy of her love was enough to make his heart skip a beat.

There was a time when he had thought he loved Rose Buchanan, but it paled compared to the affection and respect he felt for Dotty. She was truly an incredible woman. A woman who deserved more than the life of an outlaw.

"Why are you lookin' at me like that?" she whispered.

Budd could tell she was pleased, for there was a slight flush to her cheeks. "I can't help it, Dotty."

"Well, you better stop it this instant," she said with a playful edge to her voice. "The mayor has something he'd like to say."

A fork tapped against a glass of wine.

"Now, I would like to thank everyone for attending this gathering," Mayor Thomas said to the crowd. He raised his glass and stared directly at Budd. "This night is in honor of Budd Mansfield, a fearless hero who was willing to lay down his life to defend our beloved city."

A spattering of applause followed the mayor's words. "Though we are safe for now, our enemy is still out there. And Budd Mansfield has once again promised a swift justice for Sacramento," he continued. "Thank you, Mr. Mansfield. And good hunting."

Music played softly, and the quiet whispers returned.

Budd felt the heat of his embarrassment crawl up his neck and settle on the tips of his ears. He adjusted his tie with clammy hands. The mayor's dig at his past failures didn't go unnoticed.

Budd waited for the mayor to return. Mayor Thomas joined Budd and Dotty at the head of the table. Across from Budd were Douglas and Rose Buchanan. He saw the disapproval in Rose's gaze, a look that used to cut Budd like a knife, but... he found himself not caring about her opinion.

He ignored the pointed glares each time Dotty brazenly took his hand and the quiet scoffs of indignation when he brushed a curl out of Dotty's eyes. Rose Buchanan was part of his past, but he refused to allow her narrow-minded views to taint him any longer.

Dinner was full of foods Budd had trouble pronouncing. He much preferred a plate of mutton and potatoes from the inn. Still, he shoved his food down with as much grace as he could muster, for Dotty's sake, and pasted on a smile each time someone attempted to speak to him. They cleared the table after dessert.

It was all too much. Budd waved down his men and pulled Dotty out to the quiet of the back garden. Blake, Steven, and Evan greeted Dotty with smiles and impish winks.

Budd gave them a moment to settle down before he spoke. "I'm going to the Old Mill," he announced. "It's as good a place as any to start the search."

"Are you out of your mind?" Evan sputtered.

Blake lit the end of a cigar and shrugged. Steven crossed his arms over his chest and cocked his left brow in confusion. Dotty—well, Dotty was as displeased as Budd would have guessed. She thoroughly disliked the idea of him returning to such a dangerous place.

"Honestly, Budd, can I not convince you to change your mind?" she asked.

"No," he replied. "I'm not crazy, and I've made my decision. Going back is the only way to track Eagleson down.

Once I've figured out how he escaped, I can find a trail that'll lead me right to him. I just need to know that all of you are with me."

"Always," Steven said without hesitation. "It's just we barely made it out of there last time, and who knows if any of the bandits survived? There might just be another fight waitin' for us there.

Word is soon to spread that the Old Mill is up for the takin', and any gang in the region would be foolish not to grab that opportunity."

Budd nodded along as he listened to Steven. He understood their worries. He had had as many himself. But there was nothing any of them could have said or done that would change his decision. "I appreciate your concerns, I really do. But I have to do this."

"Where do we start?" Evan sighed.

Budd smiled and clapped his partner on the arm. "We ride for Yosemite Valley, head back to the Old Mill, find out how Ripley Eagleson escaped the battle, and track him down. After that, we arrest him and throw him in a cell until there's a trial. At no point is he to be left unattended. One of us stays with him at all times. I know he's persuasive, but I trust all of you."

Chapter 14

The Old Mill

Though the bodies had been cleared, and the storm had washed away the charred earth, the courtyard still held the stench of death. Budd wasn't sure if it was his memory of the place or reality, but he could hardly stomach the sight of the burned wood strewn about after the explosion.

He hoped that, like many places, the Old Mill would eventually fade into a forgotten memory for everyone who had stepped foot on the cursed land. Budd prayed quietly under his breath as he lightly stepped around the courtyard. His boots sank ever so slightly into the mud.

In his mind, Budd worked his way through what he had seen of the fight. Ripley Eagleson had disappeared from sight after the explosion. Budd had looked everywhere for the gang leader, but it seemed like Eagleson had vanished. Impossible.

He traced his steps one terrible memory at a time until he had made his way back into the loot room. Something was different. The safe that had been at the center of the back wall had been pushed aside, revealing an opened metal grate.

"Where do you think it leads?" asked Evan.

Blake, Steven, and Dotty shared matching looks of intrigue. They huddled around Budd, peering over his shoulder as he crouched down to get a better look.

"I think it leads to the river," Budd answered. "I can hear rushing water. I'm going to follow the tunnel. You four stay here and keep looking. We'll meet up in Timber." He went back to his horse and fetched his lantern. Budd lit the oil and climbed through the entrance of the tunnel while the others got to work searching the grounds of the Old Mill.

The tunnel was damp and smelled of rotted fish, but it was large enough that Ripley Eagleson could have easily slipped through. Water dripped onto Budd's hat, and he groaned in disgust. He followed the tunnel for what felt like an eternity.

The lantern fizzed out just as the tunnel tapered off into the shallows of a riverbank. Budd hopped up onto the shore and spotted a set of deep tracks. The boot marks were staggered, as if someone had limped off somewhere further west. He pushed aside some underbrush and pine needles, revealing even more tracks.

Budd stepped carefully through the forest, trying his best not to muddle the trail. He was led to the remnants of the camp where Evan had set up the explosions.

The camp had been abandoned in a hurry because of the fires, but one set of tracks was much newer and more defined than the rest. They veered off to the right before being replaced by a set of hoof marks. The possibility that the tracks belonged to Ripley Eagleson's horse was high enough that Budd trekked back to the Old Mill to fetch Ivory.

They rode west, following the trail until it went cold outside of Timber. Budd felt that familiar swell of disappointment bubble up inside of him until he saw a large black stallion that looked a lot like the horse Ripley Eagleson favored. The horse trotted around in the public corral with three other horses. Budd hurried over to the livery man and asked to see the saddle belonging to the stallion. The kind man led Budd into the stables and pointed out a finely crafted leather saddle.

There was only the one saddle bag. Budd paid the man for his help and rifled through the bag. Beneath oatcakes and a mane brush was a scrap of paper with the name of the saloon scribbled on it. Budd put everything back into the saddle bag.

"How long has this horse been here?" he asked the worker. "And when is the owner expected to return?"

The man scratched at his head and replied, "Storm has been here for about three days now. But I usually care for him through the week or even an entire month."

Budd nodded as he smiled politely. "Thank you, sir." He took his time as he walked to the saloon, glaring over his shoulder every few paces to make sure he hadn't been followed.

Budd removed his deputy badge and tucked it away safely into his satchel before he shouldered his way through the swinging doors. His eyes slid from one menacing face to another as he stepped inside. None of those faces belonged to Ripley Eagleson or his men.

"Good afternoon," Budd muttered to the bartender. "Take any orders from Ripley Eagleson today, Bill?"

"Ordered a bottle of brandy a few days ago." The burly man wiped a foggy glass with a greasy rag, eyeing Budd suspiciously. "Haven't seen him since."

"What room is he staying in?"

Bill set the glass aside and tossed the rag over his shoulder. He leaned over the bar and met Budd's gaze squarely. "You know I can't tell you that."

"You've told me valuable information before," Budd replied in a low whisper. "How much is it going to cost me to get into that room?"

There was a touch of hesitance in Bill's expression, but it wasn't strong enough to diminish the dollar signs that flashed in the bartender's eyes. "Fifty."

Budd growled low in his chest and reached into his satchel. He only had about a hundred dollars left from the last wages he earned through Pratt & Dempcy. "Twenty," he countered. "And I tell the new sheriff to look the other way on that little moonshine operation your brother has up north."

Bill's face turned a shade of red that looked slightly painful. Still, the bartender accepted Budd's terms and handed over the spare key to Ripley Eagleson's room. Budd's heart pounded fiercely as he walked up the stairs toward the long corridor that led to the rented bedchambers. Each step made his legs feel like he was walking through quicksand.

Before he knew it, he stood in front of Ripley Eagleson's door. Budd pushed the key into the lock and turned it with a flick of his wrist. The door swung open with a squeak.

***

January 1881

Sacramento, California

The new year had brought festivities that brightened the hearts of every man, woman, and child in the city. But nothing compared to the excitement that was brought on by the elections held at city hall. The people of Sacramento were eager to put aside the harrowing days of the past year and elect a new sheriff.

Marshal Greene and Mayor Thomas had watched over Sacramento as best as they could, but it was time that a lawman of the people was duly elected. Someone that Budd hoped will place the threat of Ripley Eagleson above the idealizations of politics and prestige. He respected both Ike and Dawson, but he wasn't sure either man had what it took to take on outlaws like Eagleson.

Still, he knew the city needed order, so he placed his support behind whoever was elected.

Budd and Ivory were out on their patrol when something struck him as odd. He waved over Steven, who had been posted at the front door of the city hall building. The former outlaw frowned as he walked over. Budd peered down at Steven beneath the shadows of his brimmed hat.

Steam coiled from his lips as he said, "Ripley Eagleson ain't coming…"

"But the plan you found in his room said he would be at city hall today," Steven grumbled. "We need to be here in case he tries to kill the mayor."

"But it makes little sense," Budd argued. "What does he have to gain by killing Mayor Thomas? Ripley Eagleson isn't the sort of man to do something without reward."

Steven went quiet. He rubbed at the stubble on his chin and seemed to be in deep thought as he glanced down the road at the mayor's house.

"What if you were meant to find the plan? I mean, Rip staged a bank robbery the day Black Lake burned down so we wouldn't get in the way of his bigger plans of takin' over Sacramento. What if the election is supposed to distract us from what's really goin' on in this city?"

"The man who saw Ripley Eagleson shoot Nigel Hermon swore he overheard them talking about the election," Budd said. He followed Steven's gaze to the large house at the end of the road and a shiver raced down his spine. "Stay here with Dotty and watch the mayor. I'll take Blake and Evan with me, and we'll make sure the rest of the town is safe."

Budd clucked his tongue and led Ivory down to where Evan stood on the front porch of the sheriff's office. He told Evan about his concerns, and his partner wasted no time in fetching his horse. Budd ordered the other deputies to patrol the streets in case of any suspicious activity. Dawson, Ike, Marshal Greene, and Mayor Thomas finally disappeared into city hall as a crowd formed in front of the building. Dotty and Steven flanked the front doors.

A strong wind blew, kicking up dirt on the road. Once the doors to city hall closed, Sacramento was nearly silent. Only the sound of hooves echoed off the walls of the buildings, giving the town an eerie feeling that Budd disliked. Evan and Budd met with Blake off the main road near the inn. Together, they rode along the edge of the city.

"Do you reckon Eagleson will hang for what he's done?" Blake asked suddenly.

Budd chewed the inside of his bottom lip as he thought about the question. His focus had been on catching Eagleson. He hadn't really considered what might come after. Either way, Budd supposed it was up to the courts to decide Ripley's fate. He was glad that particular responsibility rested on someone else's shoulders.

"I think he will," Evan replied. "The government is cracking down on outlaws. There's fewer of them each year. Sometimes I swear the more civilized the west becomes, the less they need men like us. We are too... untamable. No outlaws means no men needed to hunt them."

"Nah, I think there will always be outlaws," Budd mumbled. "Folk might call them something different or try to hide the fact that the world doesn't change much just because they keep building cities. But people will always want what they don't have. That sort of greed doesn't just disappear overnight."

"Tell that to the Pinkertons," scoffed Blake. "They believe they can rid the world of no-good, dirty lawbreakers."

Budd chuckled. He turned Ivory down the main road and passed by the patrolling deputies. He tipped his hat to them, carrying on as the hours passed. The first round of elections came to a close, with Mayor Thomas winning for the third year in a row. Sacramento became livelier as people milled from one place to another before they returned to city hall.

"What are we doin' out here, Budd?" Blake sighed. "We should be downtown with drinks in our hands and women in our laps."

"He's right," said Evan. "We looked around, and Ripley Eagleson ain't nowhere to be found. Let's just head back toward the Parlor Room."

Budd shook his head. He knew something was wrong, that there was more to Ripley Eagleson's plan than the letters had said. Eagleson's plot to destroy Pratt & Dempcy's hold on California had been successful. His plot to take Sacramento, however, had been foiled by Budd and his men.

The only thing Ripley Eagleson had left to fight for was his freedom. But where did the mayor come in?

"No, not until we know for sure." Budd tugged on the reins. "Let's do another round before we give up. Sacramento deserves our best work," he told the others. "I would hate for Eagleson to get the jump on us again—"

The sound of breaking glass pulled Budd's attention away from the conversation. It had come from over by the mayor's house.

Chapter 15

Sacramento, California

The bell chimed at city hall, signaling the end of the first election. Ripley Eagleson pulled his mask up and crept over to the mayor's house. He stayed low and out of sight of the road as he moved closer to the wall. His hand brushed along the bricks, feeling for any deep grooves where his fingers might fit.

Once he got a good grip, Rip climbed for the second floor of the house, where one window remained open. Charles stood beneath Rip as he waited for the signal to follow.

Rip clutched the windowpane and hoisted himself up. Pain lanced through his body. He tumbled through the opening and slumped to the floor. Rip's face went pale, his hand clutched at the wound on his side. His fingers trembled against the bandages.

He coughed raggedly, tasting that metallic tang of blood on his tongue. Rip swallowed down his pain and pushed to his feet. He hobbled across the floor. Each step felt as though it might be his last, but eventually he made it to the other side of the room. He stood in what looked to be a bedchamber. Rip blinked his eyes rapidly to clear the fog from his vision.

Once the nausea subsided, he pushed open the door and listened for any sign of servants. Not a sound echoed through the empty halls of the mayor's home. Rip shuffled into the corridor and limped toward the staircase. Glass shattered to his right. He flipped his revolver out of its holster and aimed in the sound's direction. Charles climbed through the broken window without a care.

Rip smacked the outlaw and snarled, "Are you out of your mind? What if someone heard you?"

"Ah!" Charles rubbed the back of his head with dirt-stained hands. "No one heard me! Everyone's downtown for the election."

Rip rolled his eyes and yanked Charles along. They found the study just off the main entrance. The safe was hidden behind a portrait of Mayor Thomas's father.

Rip pulled the painting off the wall and laughed happily at the sight of the large safe. He stood back as Charles worked on cracking open the lock. "There's a small fortune in that safe," Rip told Charles. "Everything we've been through will be worth it once we get to Nevada."

"Then what?"

"Pardon me?" Rip asked with an arched brow.

"What happens after we get to Nevada?"

"We rebuild," he answered with utmost confidence. "We make our family strong once again, and then we teach these simple fools what it means to fear the Blood Eagles."

Charles's smile grew tenfold as he got back to work. It was clear Rip had chosen his words correctly, relieving some unspoken fears the outlaw must have had.

Rip knew he couldn't afford to lose Charles after everyone else had been captured or was otherwise dead. He was on his own for the first time in years and that... Well, that was the only thing that made Ripley Eagleson feel a pang of regret as he kept watch.

Minutes ticked by on the clock that hung on the wall, and still the safe didn't open. Rip grew impatient as he paced across the floor. He heard hooves approaching and moved over to the window. Budd Mansfield, Blake Wright, and Evan Farris rode toward the mayor's house at full speed. A furious cloud of dust bellowed behind them.

"Hurry," Rip hissed. "Budd Mansfield and his men are here now, thanks to you." He took cover in the main room of the house and aimed his weapon through the front window. Rip opened fire the second Budd Mansfield jumped down from his horse.

The men scattered like rats, dodging bullets left and right. Rip only stopped his assault to reload before he fired once again. His ruthless onslaught of bullets pelted the fence and the nearby trees with lead.

Budd Mansfield returned fire. He shot with a speed and accuracy that Rip admired, even as it infuriated him.

Rip pressed his back to the wall and glared at Charles— who had abandoned the safe. "Get back to work on that lock, or so help me, I will hand you over!" he snarled over the gunfire. "Don't you be a coward now, Wright! Get that gold, or we are not getting out of here alive."

Rip gritted his teeth against the pain and lifted himself to his feet. He then hobbled into the dining room and hid beneath the long table.

"Come out, Eagleson!" Budd Mansfield shouted. "It's only a matter of time before deputies surrounded this place."

Just then, Rip heard the lock on the safe pop open. Charles stuffed the gold and cash into a small purse before he tossed it to Rip. They crawled across the floor to the back door of the mayor's house.

Charles helped Rip stand, but a stray bullet caught him in the back. Rip cursed as Charles dropped dead beside him. Mansfield and his men followed close behind, but Rip made it to Storm just in time.

The large stallion lurched forward and darted down the road. Bullets flew past Rip's head as he clutched the reins with a white-knuckled grip. Thunder rumbled through the valley, but instead of rain, snow fell from the heavens.

Rip rode hard, speeding along the dirt roads as if the devil himself were on his trail. Suddenly, something hard hit him across the back and knocked him out of the saddle. He hit the ground so hard that he bounced and rolled down toward the ravine.

Budd Mansfield had thrown himself into Rip without caution. He had abandoned his horse and his sanity hoping to catch him.

Rip coughed harshly and spat blood onto the ground. "You just don't know when to quit, do you? I should have killed you the day you rode into California."

***

Budd rolled onto his knees in the mud. He heaved and gasped for air, trying to see past the dark spots that danced in his vision. Ripley Eagleson recovered quicker than Budd had expected and kicked Budd in the side. He fell over, landing on his wounded shoulder.

Budd ripped the sling off and shoved to his feet. He stood at his full height and lifted his hands in a fighting stance. "You should have killed me," he said. "Because I won't stop until you pay for what you have done. Men like you don't deserve freedom."

Ripley Eagleson laughed uproariously. He tossed his head back and cackled like a madman.

And Budd supposed he was mad, for no sane person could have done the horrific things Rip had done.

"I won't let you live this time," Rip said gravely. "Not when I'm so close to a glorious victory. You might have been able to stop me before, but I've got nothing left to lose. And a man with nothing to lose has everything to gain."

"Surrender, Eagleson. Give up this fool's mission, and the marshal might hear your side of things," Budd panted. His lungs burned, and there was a slight hiss to his gasping breaths that worried him. But Budd refused to give up.

"Whether you end up behind bars or with a noose around your neck, there's still some time to end this with dignity."

"There's no dignity in surrendering." Rip threw the first punch. He swung and missed.

Budd sidestepped and landed a hit against Rip's jaw that was so hard his knuckles throbbed. He jumped back when Rip attempted a sneaky elbow to the ribs, and the blow only grazed him. They both swung at the same time and missed the mark.

Rip tripped and rolled for his gun. Budd dug for his own hand cannon. He fired without hesitation, and it shot the gun out of Ripley Eagleson's hand. Rip yelped and dove for the ground.

"This is sad, Rip," Budd said. He pressed his boot to Rip's back and reached for the cuffs on his belt. The ache in his shoulder intensified with every movement.

Shackles jangled loudly, echoing through the valley. The sound mingled with the passionate pleading that spilled from Rip's mouth now that he found himself at Budd's mercy. Budd clapped the outlaw in irons and dragged him away from the riverbank—and any hope of escape.

Budd whistled sharply, and Ivory galloped through the trees toward her rider. Budd patted the old mare on the side before he hoisted Eagleson onto her back.

"I can make you a rich man," Rip said. "Get me to Nevada, and we can split the loot. What do you say?"

Budd ignored the outlaw and unclasped the purse from Ripley Eagleson's belt. He pulled open the laces and saw a few large gold nuggets and a bundle of cash. Budd was no assayer, but he knew the heavy pouch in his hand held enough value that it could have rebuilt Black Lake twice over.

He thanked the Lord he wasn't the sort of man easily swayed by false promises and wealth. With love and friendship in Budd's life, he saw little use for money. He had enough money to get by, and that was all he needed.

"Do you really think I would have chased you all over the territory if I was after money?" Budd scoffed. "All I want—all I have ever wanted—is justice. I don't care how much I lose in the process. This is the right thing to do."

He tucked the purse into his satchel before he climbed into the saddle and secured the shackles to the saddle horn with a bit of rope. It was just in case Rip got any brilliant ideas about trying to escape. "I have been shot, stabbed, beaten, blown up, and bribed. None of it was enough to change my mind about taking you down."

"You think this is the right thing to do? That this is justice? Well, what about my justice, huh?" Rip pounded his fist against Budd's back petulantly. "I was wronged first!"

"Are you talking about the so-called disagreement that happened between you and Mr. Thayer when he caught you stealing from Pratt and Dempcy?" Budd shook his head and sighed at the pathetic tactics Ripley Eagleson had lowered himself to.

All outlaws were the same when they were captured. They all attempted to bargain their way out of the shackles, no matter how shameful it seemed. "Because I heard all about that and I think—"

"My sister needed me! My mother was ill. We had no father to look after us," Rip argued in a shrill, obnoxious voice that grated against Budd's nerves. "You wouldn't understand the sacrifices I've made in the name of my family."

Budd ignored Rip as though he were any other outlaw in shackles. He spurred Ivory on, turning her back toward the city as they rode along the path.

Budd had spent so many restless nights thinking about the day he captured Ripley Eagleson. So much so that he felt numb now it finally came to pass. There was no excitement or relief. In fact, Budd half expected another miraculous escape from the worthless criminal. But all he got was the same story he had heard a hundred times from other men who had attempted to outsmart the law.

"You made things worse," Budd said. "It doesn't matter what you did in the beginning. The problem is you did bad things instead of taking responsibility for your actions."

The rest of the ride back to Sacramento was in silence. Ripley Eagleson must have known Budd was the one man in the west who couldn't be bought.

No, Budd Mansfield was a proud man who had never once taken a bribe. And he had gone up against outlaws so fierce that bounty hunters and lawmen alike hadn't the courage to fight back.

Budd once thought Ripley Eagleson was an outlaw to be feared. Instead, it seemed, Ripley Eagleson was just as scared as his victims had been.

Chapter 16

Rip was dropped on the ground like a sack of potatoes. The door slammed shut with a rattle, and he found himself staring up at the two Pinkertons, Marshal Greene, and Budd Mansfield.

Beside them was the reinstated Sheriff Dawson, who looked as though he would have liked nothing better than to string Rip up for the hangman's noose himself. While Rip was surrounded by his enemies, he was not alone. In a cell near the back of the jailhouse sat Hector Vasquez and Isiah West. They avoided his gaze as he sat up against the wall.

"I need a doctor," Rip said around wheezing breaths. He lifted his shirt and stared down at the bloodied bandages around his middle. "Unless you boys don't want me making it to trial. Wouldn't be the first time a group of men took the law into their own hands. After all, that was how my gang started."

"Why don't you tell us a little more about your operation first?" Budd Mansfield said, earning him more than a few glares from the other lawmen. "Starting with how you found so many bandits to work for you."

"I have… allies." Rip gingerly touched the area around his wound and winced. "People who don't want to see the west become more civilized than it already is."

"So, your plan was to take over Sacramento and turn it into a bandit outpost?" one of the Pinkertons asked.

Rip shook his head and sighed. "My plan was to destroy Pratt and Dempcy for what they did to me, to rule over the roads and the trade so that cities like Sacramento would be beholden to me.

But when Budd Mansfield kept getting in my way, the plans had to change. I wanted Sacramento to be mine. I deserved it. After all, it was my money that made Elliott Thomas mayor. It was my money that helped to build this city into what it is today."

"The people are what make Sacramento the city it is," Budd Mansfield said. "No amount of blood money can change that."

Rip leaned against the wall and pulled himself up. He moved over to the bars that separated him from the lawmen. "Those same people you defend turned on you the second I told them to. They respect money, not honor, Mr. Mansfield. Heroes fade as the days pass, but outlaws… outlaws die as legends."

"Is that what you want?" Budd asked as he stepped closer. "Do you want to die a legend? Because I doubt people will remember the name Ripley Eagleson after your body drops from the gallows. Beatrice agreed to help return the stolen loot to its rightful owners. Not even she will mourn your passing."

"Who are you to judge me?" Rip snapped. He grabbed the front of Budd's shirt through the bars. The others jumped to their feet, but Mansfield held them at bay. Rip released the deputy, only to slam his fist into the man's smiling face.

Mansfield shook off the punch and wiped his busted lip onto the sleeve of his coat. "I'm the man who finally took you down. And I plan to see this through to the end."

Something inside Rip broke. He looked down at his hands that were balled into fists at his sides and stumbled back. He caught himself before hitting the floor and held onto the cell wall for balance as the room spun dangerously.

Everything suddenly felt like it was too much for Rip to handle. Beatrice had betrayed him. His men were either dead or deserters. He was truly, undeniably alone.

"What you're feeling now is guilt," said Mansfield. "It'll only get worse from here on out unless you confess and repent. Seek forgiveness from God because not one of us will give it to you." The deputy took a seat beside the Pinkertons and hung his head in disappointment.

"You wanted to get to Nevada," Sheriff Dawson said. "What would you have done if Budd hadn't caught you?"

"Salt Lake City. I'm not wanted around those parts, and there's an assayer looking to buy gold," Rip answered. "After that, I was planning on going down to Texas and rebuilding the Blood Eagles."

A string of Spanish curses and vile words came from Hector's cell. Though Rip had never learned the language, it was clear to him that Hector was less than pleased with the turn of events that had taken place. "You crook!" Hector shouted. "Everything we did for you, and you repaid us by taking the loot for yourself?"

Even Isiah West had a dejected look upon his face as he stood beside Hector. The two outlaws paced the length of the cell like caged beasts. There was no doubt in Rip's mind that the distance between the cells was the only reason he was still able to draw breath.

Hector or Isiah would have attempted to kill him, and there was no use in Rip pretending otherwise. He was out of lies, out of excuses.

Dawson banged on the cell. "Quiet!" he barked. The lawman moved to the door of Rip's cell and gave him a warning look. "You keep talking."

"Why did you kill Nigel Hermon?" asked the second Pinkerton—who had been quiet up until that point.

Rip remembered the man's name had been Smith. Lucas Smith, he reminded himself. "Well, Nigel worked for me," Rip revealed. "He was supposed to hold off the election for another week and then become sheriff. But he forgot his place and needed to be made an example of."

Budd Mansfield stared around the room as if he questioned whether or not he trusted the men beside him. Rip grinned wickedly and reveled in the uncertainty in the man's gaze. There was still hope.

Perhaps all was not lost, Rip thought to himself. Where there was doubt, there was room for him to plot his escape. With or without Hector and Isiah, Ripley Eagleson was determined to fight for his freedom.

***

Budd waved the doctor away and pulled his shirt back on. He had been shot in the same shoulder twice by his enemies, and the doctor was concerned it might never heal properly. Budd felt a twinge in his joints and groaned.

His shoulder hurt something fierce, but there was a lot of work that he wanted to do. Ripley Eagleson's capture shined a light on Sacramento, revealing there had been corruption within the city officials that Budd just simply couldn't ignore.

"Uh oh," Dotty said from the doorway. She leaned against the wall, hip cocked and a sultry smile upon her beautiful face. "You got that look about you, Budd Mansfield."

"What look?" he asked sheepishly.

Dotty chuckled and sauntered over to the side of the bed. She toyed with the button at the neck of his shirt and replied, "It is the sort of look that tells me you've got your mind made up. So much so that no amount of my persuasive words will make any difference."

"Is that so?" Budd fought back a smile and lost. He reached out and ghosted his hand over her wrist. Just the small touch was enough to set him ablaze.

Dotty was wild and free thinking. She was nothing like Rose Buchanan, and that made him love her even more. She shivered as he rubbed the pale skin of her wrist with his thumb.

Evan entered the room. "Hey, Budd, I just—"

Budd jumped away from Dotty in the blink of an eye. He cleared his throat and pointedly ignored the insufferable grin that spread across Evan's face. Dotty, however, finished buttoning Budd's shirt as if Evan hadn't interrupted the moment that had sparked between them.

Budd knew it was a fool's errand to try to tell Dorothy Valentine that anything she did was considered unseemly. It was a simple matter of fact that Dotty cared very little about what was proper. It was yet another reason why Budd admired her.

He stood up from the bed and showed the doctor to the front door, shoving past Evan in the process. Once he was alone, Budd massaged away the ache that had lingered after his examination. He hated the sling, but it relieved some of the pain, so he awkwardly slung it over his head and secured the knot.

Dotty and Evan soon joined him in the entrance corridor. Dotty opened her mouth to speak, but a knock came at the door to silence her words. Budd opened the door and felt as though he had been hit in the gut.

Howard Thayer stood upon the front porch with his head bowed and his hands gently folded in front of him as if he were a beggar. "Please, Budd…," Mr. Thayer began. "Please forgive me for what I've done. I never intended t-to besmirch your good name."

Budd stood stunned by his former employer. He placed a hand on Mr. Thayer's arm. "You were hurt and confused," he said. "Even I would have thought the worst, given the circumstances."

"But I should have trusted you! Trusted that you were an honorable man." Mr. Thayer pushed his hand out in front of himself. "Can you ever forgive me?"

Budd accepted the handshake and nodded his head. He would have eventually visited Mr. Thayer on his own, but it spoke volumes about the man who had made that leap first. Budd respected Howard Thayer, and he hoped one day Pratt & Dempcy might have the hope of rebuilding. But running a stagecoach company and building the railroads meant dealing with all sorts of people.

Bandits being one of them. Which, Budd knew, Pratt & Dempcy hadn't been prepared for. So he shook Mr. Thayer's hand once more and said his farewells to the man and the company.

And though Budd wore a deputy's badge, he never quite thought of himself as a lawman or bounty hunter. He found himself wondering what he wanted out of life. "Do you two ever think about the future?" he asked Dotty and Evan. "About what you want to do when this is over?"

Dotty blushed wildly. She glanced down at her slippers and toyed with the cuff of her sleeve. "I-I suppose I ain't given it much thought," she stammered. Though it seemed as if that wasn't entirely the truth. Dotty looked like she had given the future a lot of thought and—for some reason—that made Budd nervous. She met his gaze finally and said, "Golly! I guess I'll have to stick around Sacramento long enough to figure that out."

Evan, on the other hand, snapped his fingers with a triumphant expression on his face. "Aha! I got it! I'll work hard on earning the people's trust and run for sheriff come next election."

Budd knew the Wright brothers, Blake and Steven, both wanted nothing more than to follow him on his next grand adventure. To live on that fine line between outlaw and lawman that Budd had often found himself in.

But Budd wasn't sure what he wanted. Perhaps time could have offered a bit of clarity, but he was far too impatient to wait. "I want to start my own stagecoach company," Budd announced. "Something small and just for travel through the region, but… yeah, I think that's what I want to do."

"If anyone can keep people safe, it's you, Budd," Dotty said with a beaming grin. "I think that's a lovely idea."

Budd found himself blushing beneath her praise. He cleared his throat and rubbed the back of his neck. "I might have to buy and fix up Mr. Thayer's old stagecoaches, but I think I could make that happen."

"Good for you, Budd," Evan replied as he clapped Budd on his good shoulder. He then kissed Dotty on the cheek and headed off to work for the morning. After all, he was once again a deputy of the law.

That left Budd and Dotty alone in the awkward silence of the entrance corridor.

Chapter 17

En Route to Reno, Nevada

Rip awakened in the back of a wagon, miles from the city, with no recollection of how he got there. The shackles around his wrists and ankles jangled as he sat up on the bench. Hector Vasquez and Isiah West sat across from him with those same murderous looks in their eyes.

Sunlight filtered through the cover on the wagon, illuminating his face with its warm rays. Rip squinted and peered past the light toward the rider on the horse who watched him like a hawk.

Budd Mansfield.

Rip scooted across the bench and pulled open the cover a bit more. He smiled at Budd Mansfield as if he weren't terrified of going to trial. In truth, Rip had lost so much of himself, and everything he had built, that there was only fear left. And that fear festered inside him like nothing he had ever experienced before. The only thing that kept him from breaking was the knowledge that he had nearly broken Budd Mansfield.

"I used to be against killing, you know," Rip told Mansfield. "My gang was honorable. We only robbed those who had more than enough to give, and we never hurt a woman or child."

"John Pepper killed the first witness and knocked his wife unconscious," Mansfield growled. "On your orders."

"John's behavior was unpredictable. You can hardly blame me for his antics." Rip jangled the shackles once more. "Now, are these truly necessary? There's no way for me to escape out here."

"They're more than necessary," said Mansfield. The rider turned his mare off to the side. He only took his eyes off Rip for a split second as he spoke with his travel companions, but it was just long enough for Rip to come up with a plan.

Rip closed the cover and leaned closer to Hector and Isiah. "Be angry at me all you like, but follow my lead if you want to get out of here." He stood up and moved to the opposite bench. A voice shouted for them to quiet down, and Rip ignored it. He pointed to the other side of the wagon and said, "On my count, we throw ourselves against the side of the wagon to knock it off balance. They're taking the road through the forest. We should be coming along the side of the mountain soon."

Hector nodded along with Rip's explanation. "We knock the wagon off balance, and it goes over the side. But what's to keep us from killing ourselves?"

"We either die free or we die by the rope, boys. Let's do this."

Rip held his hand up to count off three, and the outlaws tossed their weight to the other side of the wagon. The wheels groaned as it tilted. Rip braced his legs against the bench and gripped the chains tight. They rolled, hitting every ridge along the mountainous terrain.

The wagon bounced as it rolled, and Rip felt every jostle down to his bones. There was a moment where he blacked out. He blinked open his eyes, surprised to find the wagon had stopped halfway down. Rip already heard the horses approaching. He lay on the floor of the wagon and pushed with everything he had.

The wagon rocked slightly before it tilted once more. Down they went until it crashed into a cluster of trees. Rip pulled himself up and stumbled from the wreckage. Hector climbed out of the wagon behind him. Isiah was unconscious, lying against a rock.

"Leave him," Rip said. "He isn't one of us."

***

The horses whined loudly. Marshal Greene barked orders to the other deputies while Budd broke off from the group. He rode to the edge of the cliffside and stared down the rocky terrain, tracking the path the wagon had taken.

Off to the north end of the trail was a small path that led to the valley below. Budd clucked his tongue and steered Ivory toward the path without hesitation. Steven and Blake Wright followed close behind.

"Where are you going?" asked the marshal.

"After Eagleson," Budd answered without even a glance over his shoulder.

"They couldn't have survived that drop. Come back here, Mansfield."

Budd ignored the marshal. He saw a small creek not far from a clearing in the woods and knew in his gut that was where Eagleson was headed.

"Keep your eyes sharp," Budd told Blake and Steven. "They could be hiding anywhere."

Steven pulled up beside Budd and said, "They won't get far in those chains."

Budd hoped his friend was right. After everything it had taken to finally get Ripley Eagleson in cuffs, he refused to let the outlaw escape. Too many families had been torn apart for Budd to allow Eagleson to go free.

He eased his way along the path and guided Ivory with a gentle hand. The mare trotted slowly, balancing on a narrow curve that was barely wide enough for one horse to make it through. Underbrush and dry rubble broke off and fell down the steep drop, echoing off the rock faces as it hit the ground.

A noise came from nearby shrubs and Budd lifted his rifle. "Come on out," he called. "No use in running now. There's nowhere for you to go."

Isiah West crawled out of the bushes with his wrists still clapped in irons. Steven hopped off his horse and dragged the outlaw onto his stallion with his lip curled in disgust. Blake and Budd continued down the path and found the remnants of the wagon.

Shards of splintered wood and torn cloth covered the area. One of the wheels continued to turn, though the wagon was on its side. But there were footprints that led to a small clearing beyond the trees.

Budd and Ivory sped up. They broke through the tree line, with Blake not far behind. There, in a small patch of tall grass, was Ripley Eagleson and Hector Vasquez making one last run for the river. Budd spurred Ivory on and dashed toward the outlaws. He pulled ahead and cut off their path. "Enough, Eagleson!" Budd snapped. "Give yourself up!"

"You'll have to kill me first!"

Budd slid down from his horse and lined his sights up with the bandit leader's chest. "Don't tempt me. After all you've put me through, I just might take justice into my own hands."

Epilogue

February 1881
Sacramento, California

The scent of coffee wafted through the air as Budd poured himself a cup. He enjoyed the dark aroma that filled his home almost as much as the lingering notes of rose that he smelled the second Dorothy Valentine stormed past him. He couldn't help the smile that came to his lips as she fussed around the kitchen to prepare his breakfast.

Budd set his cup aside and placed a hand on her hip to steady her frantic movements. A pretty pink blush stole across her cheeks, and Budd knew he was done for.

"Marry me," he said without thinking. But it was too late to take them back.

Dotty whirled around and blinked up at him as though he had suddenly grown a second head.

Budd self-consciously rubbed the back of his neck and shrugged. "Marry me," he repeated, though he knew he meant every word the first time.

"I-I don't know what to say, Budd…" She set the pot on the worktable and dusted her floured hands off onto her apron. "Are you sure?"

He thought about it for a while and stepped closer to Dotty. She had never been more beautiful to him than she was at that moment. "I've never been more sure in my life."

Budd grasped her chin, tilted her head back, and pressed a gentle kiss to her lips.

He felt her shock in the rigidness of her limbs before she melted against him like butter on a hot summer's day. When he pulled away, he noticed her eyes were shut and a wistful expression had come over her face.

"I take that as a yes," Budd chuckled.

Dotty swatted at his arm and snapped out of her daze. She fanned herself with one hand and took his hand with the other. "Of course I'll marry you," Dotty said. "Only a fool would think I don't love you, Budd Mansfield. I've tried my best to give you space, and I'm glad I did… but I won't be able to stand another month apart."

"Then, let's get married on Sunday. Before God and everyone else in the city." He squeezed her hand reassuringly, but he felt her pulling away.

Dotty stepped back and folded her hands gently in front of her. "What about the trial?"

"What about it?" he asked in confusion.

"I know you won't let yourself be happy until you know for certain," she said. "You walk to get the paper each day, and it kills you not to know whether they charged Ripley Eagleson for his crimes. You might not like politics, but—"

"I'll check again today." Budd said as he reached for his coffee once more. "I'll do it right now if you want me to. Whatever it takes to make you mine."

Dotty took the coffee from his hand and set it beside her pot. She placed her hands on her hips and gave him a look that said he wouldn't be having breakfast until he did as he promised. Budd sighed heavily and kissed her cheek. He grabbed his coat from the back of a chair in the dining room and left without another word.

The city was buzzing, and Budd Mansfield felt as though he couldn't breathe. He walked along the wooden planks of the sidewalk, watching with keen eyes as folks passed him by in their wagons. His heart raced wildly.

The young boy selling the daily news waved him down. He tossed the boy a coin and accepted the newspaper. They had printed advertisements and outlandish stories in black ink, sprawling across the pages. Budd was only interested in one.

Near the middle of the paper was a headline about Ripley Eagleson's trial. Budd scanned the page with his eyes and read that Eagleson had been hanged in Reno after the trial had ended. He took a deep breath and exhaled slowly, feeling as if the weight of the world had been lifted off his shoulders. Budd rolled the paper up and tucked it into his satchel.

The End

Would you consider leaving a review on Amazon? It would be appreciated.

More westerns are in the works.